FOREVER CHARMED

FOREVER LOVED BOOK ONE

L. J. HAWKE

ISBN: 978-1-7345947–1-3

✿ Created with Vellum

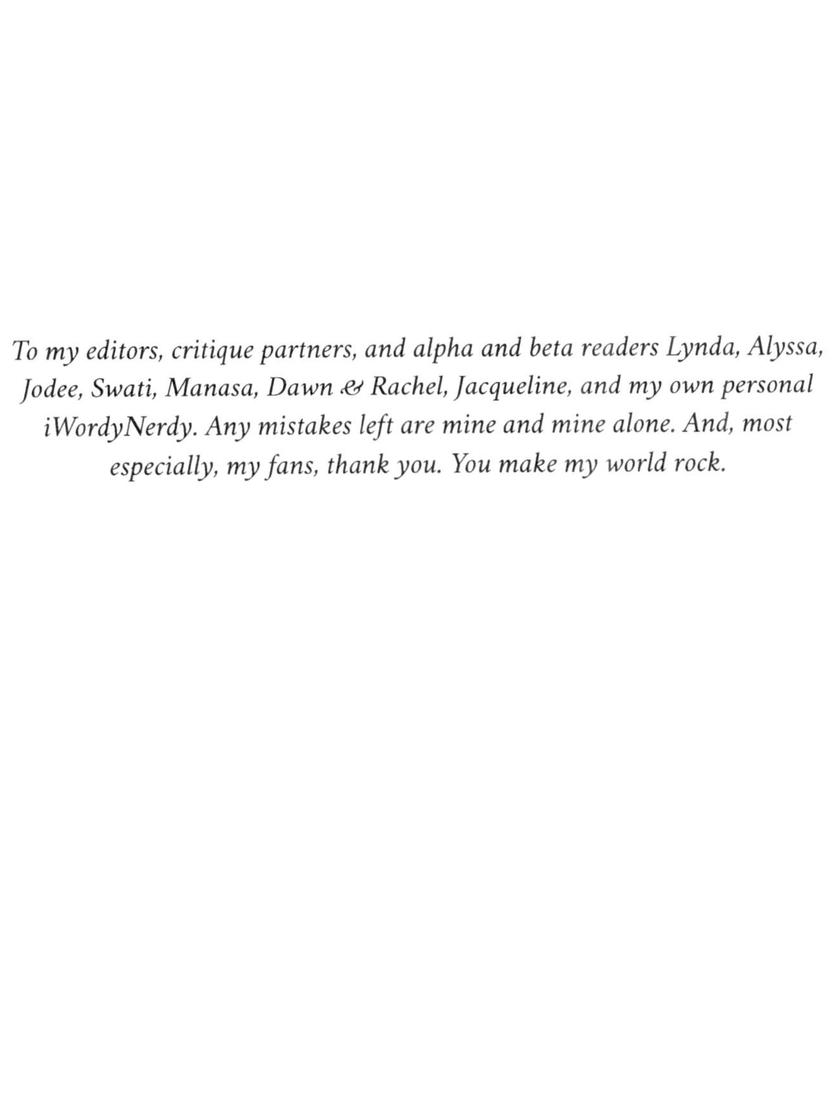

To my editors, critique partners, and alpha and beta readers Lynda, Alyssa, Jodee, Swati, Manasa, Dawn & Rachel, Jacqueline, and my own personal iWordyNerdy. Any mistakes left are mine and mine alone. And, most especially, my fans, thank you. You make my world rock.

PROLOGUE: PARTY TOWN

Parties raged across campus. Students rejoiced at the end of exams, having turned in their papers and projects and defended dissertations. They'd received their diplomas in the sweltering heat. The next day would be the end of it; students and parents would head out, diplomas and luggage in hand, staggering under the weight of microwave ovens and sports gear. But for now, the caps and gowns were off. Now? Now was the time to par-tay.

Tania was third in line to return her cap and gown. She turned it in, signed the paperwork, hurried to her dorm past clots of students and parents hugging each other, taking pictures, shaking hands. There were cheers and a lot of laughter. Tania shoved down her pointless jealousy. She entered her dorm building, climbed the stairs, put in the code, entered her dorm room. It was time to change. She rushed to her vanity. She had to dress for the party.

Tania's mind slid back ten years to Sheriff Phillips, with his dark beard and mustache and gravelly voice. For some reason, she wasn't afraid of him. They had a few moments nearly alone, Deputy Ian leaning against the door, filling out paperwork. "Your granny's taking care of your hysterical brother. I'm going to talk fast. Tania, you listen with both ears, girl, you hear?" Tania bobbed her head. "I'm real sorry about your mama. But that woman was weak. That testimony that got your father sent to prison done broke her mind. Now, you don't go thinking any of this is your fault. Your daddy, he is a monster. We found out things that you don't know, but I will say this. You are a hero. You got away, and by doing that, you saved other girls."

The sheriff ran his fingers through his curly dark hair, then put on a ball cap that said Police on the front. "Girl, your granny is a piece of work. That woman ain't going to believe the truth, that her boy, your daddy, did some terrible things. She's all piss and vinegar, and not much else. But, believe it or not, she's better than the overcrowded foster homes in this county, which is why you're going to end up living here. So, you're going to be physically safe, at least. Do not, and let me repeat that, do not listen to a word that woman says." Tania nodded her head again. She already knew her grandma was mean and didn't believe her. Called her a liar.

The sheriff continued as if he'd read Tania's mind, which spooked her a little. "You ain't no liar. She calls you that, you just find some excuse and leave the room. Go to the library. Miss Amelia Jasper is the librarian. She is a fine lady. You stay down there, do your homework. She will probably give you some bullshit job reshelving books or some such. You do what she says, and you pocket that money. There's a hollowed-out book, *Great Expectations*, German translation. You find that book, fill it up full of your money. Don't let your grandma get any of that. Then, you graduate, get the hell out of town. You go as far as you can. Shake the dust of that place off your feet. You understand?"

Tania nodded her head again. The sheriff sighed. "I'm real sorry, but that woman is going to do the same pisspoor job raising your brother that she did for her son. Your granny's gonna love your brother more and probably turn him against you. I'm sorry about that 'cause he seems like a real good boy. You try to treat that boy good, seeing as it ain't his fault. Don't listen to one word that old bat says, blaming you for breaking up your family. You did what you needed to do."

Tania felt that same sick falling feeling in her stomach when she heard the whispers, knew that stuff was probably true. Tania had no idea what made her daddy go around the bend.

The sheriff kept talking. "You remember what I said." Heavy footsteps sounded in the hall. The sheriff put his finger to his lips. Tania put her fingers to her own lips.

Miss Amelia had been older than God, had been real close to retirement. She wore house dresses, pearls, and sensible shoes. Miss Amelia walked like something was wrong with her knees. She'd had some surgery, but it didn't take. She had woolly, gray hair on her head and a huge smile that lit up a room.

Tania slipped back to the present as she put the precious pearl earrings away in the box. Tania tried to stop herself, but she just had to listen to Miss Amelia's last message. She had seen her last in April, been up for spring break. Tania had wanted to invite Miss Amelia to her graduation in person. Tania had hoped to get her brother to come too, but he made himself scarce, made it clear that he believed Tania had broken up the family.

Miss Amelia's voice was strong on her last voice message. "Girl, you done good. You take those exams. I expect you to get a good grade. I've got something to tell you. You got to know that it's my time to shuffle off this mortal coil. My heart, you know. I'm real happy you were able to come down and see me, real glad we had some of my peach cobbler together back on the porch. I won't be here anymore, so coming down here is not going to help. I've decided to have my ashes scattered down by the pond, followed by an ice cream social at the church. There will be kids there, laughing. I have always loved the laughter of children."

Tania barked out a laugh, tears on her cheeks. The library was supposed to be quiet, but Miss Amelia did enjoy laughter there. "Don't come. Your grandma's going to take your brother, and she'll say horrible things about me 'cause it always made her jealous that someone else was raising you better. If you come, you're going to end up going to jail."

Tania snorted. Miss Amelia had been right. One bad word out of that old biddy's mouth, and Tania would have hauled off and punched her. "You graduate. You get a great reputation of what you can do. Just like my son told you, you shake the dust off your feet and go as far away as you can, thousands of miles away. I'll be with you every step of the way. My earrings are going to come to you in a little box. You wear them on your graduation day and know that I'm with you."

Tania stopped the message, realized tears were streaming down her face. She doubled over and howled. She had wanted Miss Amelia in the front row, but that wasn't how it was going to be.

Tania washed her face, put her makeup on again. Corinne and Kandace were still busy turning in their caps and gowns, giving her time to spend with Miss Amelia. Tania stowed away the earrings and the makeup. Then she walked out, made sure the door locked, then ran down the stairs and out into the summer sun.

The graduation parties were the last goodbye before everyone went on their way. She had one last night with her friends. She had to have fun, for them. They should remember laughter with each other, like giggling in a small-town library.

Tania headed past clots of students to their first stop. She spotted Kandace and Corrinne and waved. Tania Brussell and her best friends, Corinne Jackson and Kandace Walker, all wore light summer clothes and looked like jeweled butterflies. Tania wore a cobalt fluttery shirt over boy shorts in a deep teal. Her coppery skin shone with a sheen of sweat, her strawberry blonde hair pulled up with tiny jeweled butterfly pins. Corinne was in jean shorts and a red top, her hair in a French braid. Kandace's top was silver and black, with black shorts. She looked stunning, sweat making her look like a golden-red fantasy in the light.

No one from any of their families had called, written, or even sent an email or a card, let alone shown up for graduation. The three young women considered themselves sisters and had one gorgeous night ahead before splitting up. Tania was determined to enjoy every minute.

They made the rounds to say thank you and goodbye: Sigma Chi, Sigma Epsilon, Sigma Sigma, and Drama Club with an emphasis on non-toga costumes. Just outside Greek Row was The Bash with the

Society for Creative Anachronism, held across the meadow from the small Geek Squad house where the Captain's Party raged, complete with "Venusian" cocktails and people sporting blue or green skin and pointed ears.

Many people learned that girls from the holler that talk like they are from the backwoods have long memories for every slight, dismissal, rude gesture, and nasty piece of gossip followed by a "Bless her heart." They also remembered every offer of a favor and casual "We should…," invitation. To them, there were no insincere invitations. They were not afraid to show up with food, liquor, and if appropriate, candles and blankets. People lost their insincerity around the three backwoods girls; those holler girls didn't stand for it. The few who helped them, who had kind and generous spirits, they deserved a true goodbye.

Tall Tait was at Delta Gamma, an occasional volunteer at the animal shelter. The newly-graduated molecular biologist had wide shoulders and huge brown eyes. His normally smiling face was sad as he kept an eye on roomie Billy, who was getting sozzled. "Thank you for helping Corinne with the dogs," said Tania."

Tait nodded. "Least I could do."

Tania followed his eyes. "You don't have to keep watch after tonight."

Tait nodded. "I was real clear. He keeps on the way he's keeping on, his daddy won't keep paying. Now he won't graduate with us. Damn shame."

Tania nodded, and gave Tait a hug. Billy had been different, once. He had gotten both cocky and belligerent. "I'm so sorry," she said.

"Didn't know you can kill love, or respect," Trey replied. Tania had found that one out years ago. She patted Tait's arm, then said goodbye. She found her girls, dragged them back out into the hot night, then they went on their way.

Finally done with goodbyes, they walked up the wide porch steps of Sigma Delta Gamma and stumbled inside. Shan, a tiny Vietnamese woman with ultra-precise movements, was there with her entire manicure/pedicure setup where the hallway turned into the wide great room. Sigma girls flitted by with trays of martini glasses filled with fruit. It was Corrine's turn to drink. Corrine took a drink with peaches floating in it, and Tania and Kandace both had Kandace's virgin mojitos.

Tania and Corinne were doing a solid for Kandace, taking turns drinking from her pack of non-alcoholic drinks, bottles with the labels removed or scratched off. They were wildly colored; electric blue, hot pink, lime green. Kandace was clean and sober, so their drinks were non-alcoholic. Tania didn't mind; sugar made her feel fantastic after she had just run herself into the ground for exams.

Kandace didn't drink since the little drunken incident with the Jeep, the third-floor physics lab, and the six people it took to take the Jeep apart and put it back together. The bill came nearly to the price of the Jeep for the professor to have his ride taken apart, carried down two flights of stairs, and reassembled.

Tania said, "Don't get why they call this drink a virgin. None of us have been virgins for a long damn time."

"Have not one hint of a clue." Corinne tugged on her braid.

Kandace grinned. "Nope. Bobby Kennedy. Ninth grade. Pinto. Kept banging my head on that little roof."

Tania threw back her head and laughed. "Cammer Dalton. His parents' basement. Tenth grade. Fastest ten minutes of my life."

Kandace and Corinne both burst out laughing. Corinne had to put down her drink because she was laughing so hard the liquid went up her nose.

Corinne held up her hand, got herself under control. "David Meineke. Eleventh grade. Under a tree, under the stars, a bottle full of Boone's Farm strawberry wine."

Kandace sighed. "I miss Strawberry Hill. Good thing I got me a smoothie maker, or I'd die from jealousy."

"We're behind ya, sis," said Tania. "Hurry up, 'cause I want to put on chain mail and swing a sword."

"That sounds wrong somehow." Corrine wiggled her toes.

"Tell me about it," said Kandace. "Are my toes ready yet?" she asked Shan.

"Ten minutes. You good girls sit there." Shan pointed over to the right. Kandace slipped her a five, and they all moved to the window seat looking over the quad. A Butterfly Girl newbie came by with a tray of Italian sausage and potato kabobs on one side and chicken satay with peanut dipping sauce on the other.

"Thanks." Tania smiled and took the whole tray. "What? I'm hungry!" she said when Corinne and Kandace stared at her. They pigged out on skewered food and sent the tray back once they had emptied it. They finished their drinks, and a first-year took the empties.

Tania stood up "Chain mail! Let's go, ladies!"

They went out into the moonlit darkness. Crickets sang and sweat beaded their bodies in the steamy night. They lurched across the quad, laughing so loudly they disturbed the bats swooping down to pick off the mosquitoes. They took a left, and skirted the edge of the campus past student, then professor, housing to get to the Society for Creative Anachronism's practice field. They could hear the cheers, blows, and drunken catcalls from down the street.

Tania pushed aside her sadness over this being her last few bouts. The Society for Creative Anachronism didn't exist in South Korea. She skipped up to Tragen, a huge sandy-haired football player who could also swing a broadsword or mace. Tonight, he was in charge of check-ins and equipment rentals. He wore a kilt and had blood smeared across one cheek.

"I'll take chain mail, greaves, and a sword," Tania said, and handed him a crumpled ten-dollar bill.

"That rack will fit you," said Tragen, pointing to a rack of noticeably smaller armor to the right. Football and basketball players tended to take the left side, with the huge padded armor and broadswords. "You other ladies want to try?"

"We want to watch," said Kandace. Kandace and Corinne draped themselves on hay bales while Tania went to the tent to don her outfit. She came out of the changing tent in a leather bustier, silver greaves flickering in the light, a leather skirt, and sandals that wrapped up her calf. She looked like an Amazonian goddess.

Tania's first bout was hard, fast, and furious. Tania went against Claw, real name Raynette, a tiny blonde woman with a button nose and beady eyes, her hair damp with sweat. Tania's skin glowed copper in the bright moonlight. It was astonishing how quickly they moved. Claw went for hard swings, using her heavier weight to her advantage, Tania used blocks, feints, and sweeps. They rolled in the grass, came up. Tania finally blocked, then stabbed. She would have gone through Claw's side if she hadn't held herself back.

"Hold!" barked Aeger, the judge, dressed as a Roman gladiator. The twenty or so watchers cheered. Tania and Claw met, placed their greaves on both sides of each other's heads.

They hugged it out, then it was Scar's turn. Scar actually had a scar over her right eye from a motorcycle accident. Her real name was Dorothea, or Dorrie to most. She sported corded muscles from lifting swords and hay bales for onlookers to sit on to watch the bouts in her free time. She also worked with a real blacksmith and designed her own costumes.

Scar enjoyed sneaky attacks as well as blitzes. Her hair was more like Kandace's, more of a dusky red with black tips. Scar's cheekbones were sharp enough to cut, and she wore shorts under a leather sarong, along with a leather bustier in black against Tania's red. Scar held two dirks, one in each hand. They circled, then started swinging at each other.

Tania thought to herself, *It's my last night; might as well come out on top.* She took Scar on with ferocity. There were flurries of blows, feints, dodges, rolls, slides, and fancy footwork. Tania swung, rolled, stabbed, spun, and went at it again, sweat running down her back, a wild grin on her face. They were at it for almost twenty minutes before the judge declared a draw.

Both women were a bit battered and bloody. "Buy you an ale," said Tania. Scar, gasping, nodded. They sheathed their weapons and clasped greaves. They changed out of their fighting clothes, and Tania wiped herself down with a bucket of water and a sponge in the changing room. She checked each wrist and ankle carefully, but everything worked. She applied balm on her bruises and dressed, then turned in her rented equipment.

Tania and Scar bought each other some dark ale from the Society's keg on the side of the practice field. The women talked about their numerous bouts together, wished each other well, hugged it out, then Tania rejoined her friends.

Tania, Corinne, and Kandace stayed up all night. The Geeks were having an Avengers movie marathon, so they went there to relax after Tania's fight. They popped popcorn and laced the bowls with mini M&M's, and drank Mountain Dew—the soda, not the local high-octane brew. Kandace and Corinne fussed over Tania's bruises and made snarky movie commentary that kept everybody laughing.

Tania wanted Tony Stark for her pretend husband, surprising the other two. "What?" asked Tania. "You girls whining 'cause I didn't pick Captain America?"

"Thor all the way," said Kandace.

"Loki," said Corinne. They both stared at her.

"You like bad guys," said Tania. She sighed and stole popcorn from Kandace's bowl. Kandace stole more back. Tania glared at her and said, "I want my guy to be smart. Precise. A little dangerous." Kandace snorted and stole more popcorn.

They walked back down the road at dawn, past the people stumbling around in last night's party clothes, dancing to music only they could hear. They arrived at the dorm and looked at their packed things. Tania got the suitcase she had packed before graduation, stuffed it behind the seat of Corinne's ancient red truck, and went with her girls to the airport.

They found a Waffle House on the way and ordered pecan waffles, crispy bacon, and orange juice. "My entire life in a rolling bag," said Tania.

"Not much more for us," said Corinne. "'Cept for Kandace's climbing gear."

"Cliffs and cabins are our friends." Kandace sucked on orange juice.

"I hate this leaving thing." Tania tried not to cry.

"Shut your mouth, woman. These are fan-freaking-tastic waffles. And the bacon is extra crispy." Corinne grabbed a piece of bacon, bit into it with a crunch.

Tania looked at Kandace and grabbed her hand. Kandace dried her eyes and hugged Tania. Corinne finished her bacon, sighed, and hugged Tania on the other side. They wiped their tears and finished breakfast.

They got to the airport two hours before Tania's international flight. Tania did everything she learned to do in the travel videos. She took off her tiny butterfly hair clips in the bathroom and stowed them in her luggage, and put on comfortable sweats and tennis shoes, her passport safely in a case around her neck. She came back out of the bathroom ready to harass her friends. "Y'all better call, text, email," said Tania.

"I will," said Corinne.

Tania cut her eyes at Kandace. Kandace sighed, pissed at having to spell it out. "I will stay sober," she said.

Tania narrowed her eyes. "You better. Not scraping you off a damn sidewalk." Kandace's best friend in the Program, Marti, had relapsed, gotten drunk, and climbed the water tower during a hot summer night of high wind gusts before a storm hit the next day. She fell off while drunk, lapsed into a coma, and died four days later.

Corinne cringed. "Hey."

Kandace held up a hand as if swearing on a Bible. "I will stay sober and not fall off the water tower to a horrific death. Or be a stupid ass and go bungee jumping with those crazy college kids. Yeah, they're mostly old bikers at my meetings, but there are no old bold bikers."

"Cool," said Tania. They clasped hands, let go. Corinne and Kandace walked behind Tania's silver rolling bag, her computer case with its ultralight, cheap pink Walmart laptop on her shoulder. They stood with her as she scanned her passport, received an e-ticket, and went to the desk to turn in her luggage and get her boarding pass.

They walked her to the security gate. "Come back to us," said Corinne.

Tania rolled her eyes. "I'm going to South Korea, not the moon. It's got a lot of really tall buildings, and apparently it's more wired than Japan."

"Rock and rule it," said Kandace. "If I've learned any damn thing, it's that life is extremely short. Enjoy every damn minute."

"Will do," said Tania. A last hug and tears, and she went through the glass doors, a smile on her face as she walked into her new life.

HEAVEN LIFE

*T*ania had a week to move out and go...somewhere. It was three weeks before winter vacation, and only a few months into her new year-long contract. Very few schools would hire at that time of year, the same in Japan as well. Tania had to go somewhere. She decided she might as well try to find someplace warm.

Since she was days away from losing her teaching visa, Tania had to leave the country on a visa run anyway. She decided to attend a job fair in Thailand that would start in three days, edited her resumes, went to a printer to print them, and cried when she had to spend precious money that could have been spent on her massive education debts on a ticket for Chiang Mai.

She had paid off thirty-eight percent of them by living in a studio apartment she could barely turn around in and eating mostly ramen noodles, but her after-school academy where she had taught had closed suddenly when the owner's father had a heart attack. He survived, but his son closed the academy to care for him.

Tania couldn't go back to the USA, after application after application for schools all over the country were rejected. It was right before winter break. Her friends had their own new lives, and she could never go back to where she came from again. She shuddered. Except for her grandmother and brother, who both hated her, she had no real family except Corinne and Kandace. Her friends were enough; they had to be. They were in their own economic holes; she couldn't ask them to help bail her out. No, Tania had to stand on her own.

Tania thought it through and decided to apply for both education and online marketing jobs everywhere she could. She still had online marketing clients from the States, but that income wasn't anywhere near enough to pay the rent. Tania answered job website ads in various countries, including Thailand, Vietnam, Malaysia, and Indonesia. Her future was terrifying but open. Every decision she made would either bring her closer to her goals or blow up all the forward progress she had made. She hoped she was making the right decision to go to the job fair in Thailand. If she didn't get a job, she'd have to spend more money to fly back or find another job fair in Asia.

Going from icy winter to a balmy and humid climate was delightful. The plane ride to Chiang Mai was relatively short, and Tania changed into shorts and a loose shirt in the bathroom when she landed. She stuffed all of her winter clothes in the bottom of her backpack and went to catch a motorcycle taxi for her backpacker hotel. She bought sunblock and mosquito repellent at a nearby convenience store and applied both before checking in.

The next morning, Tania took a motorcycle taxi to the job fair. She was stunned to see the sheer number of people lined up outside the conference center/hotel, resumes in backpacks, briefcases, and held in clear folders. Tania perused online ads on her cell phone while waiting in line. Once inside, Tania circled the space like a shark and put in applications for both teaching and marketing but was exhausted and discouraged by the end of four hours. No interview had lasted longer than three minutes. "Happy birthday," she said to herself.

Tania took a motorcycle taxi back to her backpacker hotel, ordered lunch and some iced lime tea at a cafe, and started looking up job sites online. She spied an online ad for a specialist in internet marketing to help an import-export company working with Thai businesses. Tania applied for that job, ate her late lunch, applied for more jobs online, and got her one and only answer from the thirty-one jobs she'd applied for that day. She made an online appointment to visit the import-export business the next day.

In the morning, Tania took a *tuk tuk,* a motorcycle with a sheltered seat in back to the address. It was just north of the Nimman District, famous for providing housing and working spaces for people working online who called themselves digital nomads. There were hotels, cafes with dozens of tables with computer hook-ups and even pools and gyms, places advertising laundry washed and charged by the kilo, restaurants spilling the scents of lemongrass and lime into the air.

Tania entered the gate in the white wall that led to the building and found herself in a cool courtyard with a small fountain. She smiled looking down at the carp in the artificial pond. Tania walked over the little bridge and opened the door to the building of teak and glass. Inside the long, narrow space a Thai woman sat at a front desk, her hair perfectly coiffed, wearing a dark blue skirt and a gold, silk top. Tania was glad she'd also went with a skirt and went up and introduced herself. "I'm Tania Brussell, here to see Mr. Kaung."

"Yes, of course," said the woman in perfect English. "Please, have a seat." Tania did, smoothing her skirt.

A woman in black Capris and a coral top with a backpack on her back came out, high ponytail swinging behind her. She moved at a brisk pace, her low heels clacking on the tile floor, and slammed the door shut behind her.

"Mr. Kaung will see you now," said the receptionist, unperturbed by the woman's outburst. Tania stood up, walked back to the office, and peered in. The person standing behind the curved mahogany desk was tall, with black hair somehow layered with shimmery copper that brushed his shoulders. *Hell of an expensive dye job,* Tania thought. He wore khaki slacks and a royal blue polo shirt that brought out the copper overlaying his black hair. His coppery skin was smooth, and he had huge brown eyes. He unfolded himself from his seat, stood, and smiled gently at Tania.

"Please be seated," he said. "My name is Sanur Kaung. I would be delighted to hear more about what you do." He gestured to the two rattan seats in front of his desk. His voice was cultured, precise, with hints of both British and Australian accents.

Tania took in a breath, fought for composure. Those eyes kicked up her heart rate. "My name is Tania Brussell." She sat in one of the proffered seats. "I've been teaching as well as working on marketing, specifically social media marketing, to bring together small businesses and individuals. I know how to do ad campaigns that bring people to your website."

"Anyone can do that," said Mr. Kaung. "I need someone punctual, reliable, who doesn't live on Thai time. I may have you work with clients, find me a new receptionist, and do other things as needed. I need someone who can multitask."

"So you want me to be your office manager as well as your internet marketer?" asked Tania. "And the receptionist is leaving?"

"Yes," he said. "Leyva, the person you met at the front desk, is doing me a favor right now. She's off to a university in the United States in a week."

"How wonderful for Leyva," said Tania. "I will congratulate her on the way out."

Mr. Kaung smiled. "That's the kind of small touch that I'm looking for. This business is doing very well. Thai people and those from the surrounding countries have some excellent products, mostly furniture and art, that can be sold all over the world. It's my job to get those products out. The craftspeople who make them are working in their homes or with small manufacturing. These people deserve just as much of a chance as large businesses. With online sales, they receive most of the profit."

"And your cut?"

"Ten percent across the board. You see, I already have money. I don't need to steal money from the people that I'm trying to help."

"That's a change from how people normally do business. At least in the United States."

"You'll find the people of Thailand a bit different." Mr. Kaung smiled, then his eyes grew serious. "I will give you thirty percent over what I promised to pay in the ad if you will be my office manager as well as my internet salesperson."

"Do you need help with your website? I've looked at it, and I can think of a few improvements you can make."

Mr. Kaung raised his eyebrows. "Excellent. What exactly would you like to change?"

"Well, it's a small business. You want to really make the products shine. The colors are a little too garish, and some of the wording is a bit stilted. You want to come across as friendly while still being professional."

"And you can do that for me?"

"I can." Tania kept her voice cheerful but worked to show her competence. "I went through the Free Code Camp program, learning to program both the front and back end of websites."

"Well, once you learn Thai, you can do some translation on this end."

"It'll cost you." Tania smiled to take the sting out of her words, but she meant them.

Mr. Kaung smiled back. "I'm absolutely certain that it will. What you will need to do is bill me for your separate activities. We will compile them into a salary. For now, the base salary is thirty percent over the one in the ad, but we'll add on more when you sign the contract for your website work. You will also have an hour and a half for lunch. There's normally a two-hour lunch here, but I expect you to be back in the office before then."

"Of course."

"Have you selected an apartment yet?"

"No, I have not. I figured it was better to find a job first."

"Well then, there's a place not two blocks from here. It has a pool and is a one-bedroom apartment. It also has a small gym, a convenience store, and a laundry."

"How much a month?" Tania tried to keep the fear out of her voice. An apartment with a pool sounded expensive. She would live in a shack if she had to.

Kaung grinned. "The rent is only three hundred American dollars a month, so I will pay for that. You will be required to pay some bills, but they probably won't come to more than a hundred dollars a month."

"That sounds excellent." Tania tried not to dance in her seat. "What made you choose me so quickly?"

"You're young, you're bright, and you're not here just to see the sights. You're here to work. I read between the lines on your cover letter, and I'm sorry that your last school closed so suddenly. You've been living overseas for over a year, and it's obvious that you have a grasp of expat life." Tania nodded, and Mr. Kaung sighed. "Many of the people applying are so-called digital nomads. They're here to begin a business that they can do online and use it to travel. Expat living is not nomad living, and I don't want someone who will be here for two months and then vanish. I've made the mistake of hiring people like that, and I don't want to do it again."

Tania nodded. "I understand. I will be happy to sign a multi-year contract."

Mr. Kaung wrote something on a sticky note, pulled it off its pad, and stood. Tania stood as well. "Welcome to my company." He shook Tania's proffered hand.

"Thank you." Tania smiled at her new employer. He smelled...like paper and incense. A little dry and smoky at the same time. And that hair. She had to sneak into his calendar and find the name of his hairdresser someday.

Mr. Kaung let Tania's hand go. "I will have Leyva move back my afternoon calls. Let's get you the apartment. I take it your things are in a hotel?"

Tania was elated by the fast turn of events. "They are, Mr. Kaung. I only have one more box that can be shipped. It will be nice to get rid of all of my winter things." She granted Mr. Kaung a dazzling smile.

"That it will. Please, call me Sanur."

"Sanur?" asked Tania. "Isn't that a segment of Bali?"

"Yes, it is. My parents fell in love there."

"That sounds romantic." Tania smiled and went ahead of Sanur at his gesture.

"Apparently it was." They went to the reception desk. "Leyva, please move back my afternoon calls by thirty minutes, then alter the employment contract in these ways and leave it on your desk." He handed over the yellow note with the changes. "After that, please get yourself some lunch."

"Yes, boss," said Leyva and laughed.

"Congratulations on attending college," Tania said.

Leyva smiled, showing all her blindingly white teeth. "Thank you. Hard work gets you everywhere!"

Sanur opened the door for Tania. "Let's go." They walk the two blocks in silence because a building was under construction nearby. "Sorry about the noise. It's the price of doing business here. Things are booming in Chiang Mai, and you'll find that there is some construction nearly everywhere. It's quieter here, believe it or not. As I've said, your new apartment building has a convenience store as well as a laundromat. It's usually only a dollar or two to wash your clothes."

"Fantastic, I much prefer that. Takes up less of my time." Tania meant every word. No one in South Korea used clothes dryers. Hanging up laundry to dry in a small apartment was annoying.

They entered the lobby, and Sanur spoke fluent Thai to a beautiful young woman with a wide face wearing a blue uniform. She took them in the elevator to look at some apartments. They were shown three different apartments, each one bigger than the last. The third one had a beautiful view of a nearby park and was very quiet. "Is this one all right?" Tania asked Sanur.

"It's within budget. Housekeeping will clean your apartment twice a week; it's part of the price."

Tania looked around. There was a modular couch, a flat screen TV, a beautiful white balcony big enough to put a table and chairs out there, a bedroom a little larger than its queen-size bed, a wardrobe, a bathroom with a small rain shower, and a galley kitchen. "I love it." Tania felt like pinching herself to be sure she wasn't dreaming. This was nearly twice the size of her South Korean apartment.

Sanur regally nodded his head, then spoke in Thai. The lady smiled and handed a business card to Tania. "Please go to your hotel, check out, and move your things here," said Sanur. "Show this card to the *tuk tuk* driver, and he will get you back here. This lady will be waiting at the front desk with your key cards. The one with a red border is used to get into the apartment building, and the second one with a blue border is to enter your room. Don't lose either one, because if you lose them after hours, you will have to sleep somewhere else for the night, and then hire a locksmith to break you back in. Come back to the office when done. Can you remember where that is?"

"Two blocks that way." Tania pointed.

"Excellent. I have some paperwork to sign. Can you get back to the office in approximately forty minutes?"

"Less than that. The hotel isn't that far away."

Sanur nodded that regal nod of his again, the planes of his face opening into a small smile. They went down in the elevator, and Sanur waved down a *tuk tuk* to get to her hotel. Sanur paid the driver in advance, and the driver took her the few kilometers to the hotel. Tania asked him to wait to take her back to the apartment. It took Tania only a few minutes to check out of her hotel and soon was back at the apartment. She paid the driver a little extra, was given her entry cards, dropped off her rolling suitcase, and immediately went back to work.

Sanur had added a list of the various prices paid in Thai *baht* to Tania's contract alongside the various jobs that she would be doing. Tania used a currency exchange website to do the conversions. The salary was lower than she had been making in South Korea. But with all of her extra jobs, Tania would end up making just above her last salary. Tania did an internal happy dance, pretended poise on the outside, and signed her name on the bottom of the three-year contract.

Sanur took her to lunch, and they had shrimp dim sum and cold mint tea. "I can give you some time to acclimate yourself."

Tania shook her head. "I might as well learn the job. Shall I do some training after lunch?"

Sanur laughed. "Most people would take the afternoon off and go to the pool. I like your drive and ambition. You were certainly the best candidate for this position. I'm very pleased with my choice."

"Thank you very much. I'm delighted to be working with you."

Sanur nodded his head regally. "Likewise."

After lunch, Sanur walked Tania around the neighborhood and pointed out grocery stores, numerous restaurants, and the mall. He then took her back to the office, gave her a golden Apple laptop still in its box, and Tania started work immediately at her desk, just back from the receptionist's. Tania set up the new computer and immediately began working on the company's website. Pleased, Sanur went back to his office. When Leyva came back from lunch, she trained Tania on the phones.

Tania left at five o'clock and walked to the mall. She reveled in the air conditioning and found some delightful dim sum to eat for dinner for only about two American dollars. Then she bought things she needed, like sheets and towels. She walked to her new home, changed into her tankini, and worked out.

Afterward, Tania then took one of her brand-new large fluffy beach towels and went to the pool. She delighted in the slide of cool water over her skin, walked back and forth until she got tired, swam, then walked again. She finally got out to lay in the padded lounger and was startled at how life could change in just a moment.

⁓

The next day, Sanur closed up shop and took Tania to get her Thai visa. They waited in an interminable line in a hot office. Tania had already applied for a work visa, and now that she had a job, she needed to turn in her new employer's paperwork to receive the visa. Sanur spoke in fast Thai to the person behind the desk and showed Tania's contract. There was a lot of stamping, and then Tania got her work visa. While she was waiting, she texted Jo, her old boss, to send her things to her new Thai address, and to donate her winter clothes and heavy linens.

After rehydrating at a coffee shop with a smoothie, Tania returned to work. When she got back to the office, she realized that she couldn't be the receptionist without being able to speak Thai. She needed someone to sit in front, smile, and take phone calls. She had two choices. She could go with an agency, or she could put an ad written in English on a Thai website. Tania immediately decided against an online ad. It would bring in many people, and she would be overwhelmed with interviews.

Tania decided to go ahead and go with an agency. She specified that she needed someone with an extremely high English level. They sent a beautiful woman in a teal dress and three-inch black heels. She had long, black hair held back in a golden clip and beautifully-done makeup. The woman, who gave her name as Preet, spoke little English. She refused to type anything into the computer. Everything that Tania showed her she ignored in favor of working on her nails. "I answer the phone," she said.

"No, you don't get to sit here and do nothing in between calls." Tania narrowed her eyes at Preet. "Don't you know how to use a computer?" Theyoung woman shrugged.

Tania painstakingly showed Preet what to do on the computer and how to do it. Preet sighed and refused to pick up her pretty fingers to do anything, even fill out a form letter or message pad. Finally, incensed, Tania said, "You're fired." She paid her for a full hour of work, even though the woman had been there less than an hour. Preet made a slight grimace of distaste and swished off.

Tania called the agency and said she wouldn't be needing anyone else for now. She realized they didn't need talent; what they needed was someone they could train exactly the way that they would like. Tania searched on a website, used a translator program, and found a nearby orphanage with teens living there. She knew that she'd have a winner if she could find a teen with a high enough English level. Tania did some online research and discovered that the Thai working age was fifteen years old, and that she would have to tell the Thai labor board within fifteen days about the under-eighteen employees.

Tania got up, told Sanur she was leaving for a short time, and transferred the calls to his phone. She caught a *tuk tuk*, and soon found herself in front of the orphanage. She went to the front door and spoke to a young woman with short, choppy hair and a blank face sweeping the front steps. Tania told the woman she needed to speak to the director to see if there were any teens with very high levels of English for a job. Two girls and two boys rushed up to her and asked what the job entailed.

They brought her inside, and Tania kicked off her shoes and sat on the floor with them, as they had very little furniture, and obviously slept on the floor on mats that were piled up in the corners. Tania explained that she needed a receptionist and asked their ages. All four of them were sixteen years old. The girls spoke better English than the boys, so she decided to go with them first. She told the boys not to worry, because they would probably have other work for them later on.

The director of the orphanage came out to find out what was going on. She was short and wore a loose dress far too large for her tiny body. She had a wide, flat face and a warm smile. The teens explained in a spill of rapid Thai. "I am Mrs. Amioad. I am delighted that Achara and Kannika have found employment. Where will they be working?" Tania took Mrs. Amioad and the teen girls back to the import/export company's office via *tuk tuk*, showed the girls the reception desk, and talked about their duties and payment.

Sanur came out and introduced himself to both Ms. Amioad and the two young ladies in Thai. Sanur then took them up past the second-floor loft to the third floor, to the small apartment there. There was a studio apartment, with a large queen bed, plenty of storage, an air conditioning unit, and a small kitchenette.

The girls were extremely happy. They were in Thai school, and Tania asked whether or not the girls could go on a half day. One girl would be the morning receptionist and the other one the afternoon person. Tania also offered to pay for their online English education.

After a very quick Thai conversation with Sanur, Mrs. Amioad determined that it was a good idea for them to get a free apartment. The orphanage was crowded, the girls would be aging out of the system, and the apartment on the third floor and three meals a day came with the job. The girls would also receive an online education in English.

Tania explained that she had gone to many classes online because her small school in the holler where she grew up didn't allow her to take more advanced classes. She showed the girls the educational website and explained that she would expect the girls to be doing their homework on the computers at work when they weren't directly working with clients or had other tasks, and that the girls would have a laptop to share for their apartment.

Achara, the taller of the two, wanted to work on the morning shift. She laughed and said she was always up before the dawn. Kannika was delighted to work afternoons. Sanur showed all of his permits to Mrs. Amioad. He then started working on the relevant paperwork for the Thai government, which Mrs. Amioad signed. Sanur took the director with him to file the paperwork. On his way out, he slipped Tania a company credit card and told her to buy the girls whatever they needed, and that they were closed for the day.

Tania took the young ladies for makeovers. They all had their hair cut and got mani-pedis. Tania supplied them with tea and fruit juices and took them out for noodles and chicken. Then Tania took them shopping for simple dresses and sandals, which made both girls smile hugely and laugh behind their hands. Then they got housewares; a microwave oven, a rice cooker, bowls, plates, chopsticks, and a teapot at the mall for the girls and for Tania.

They hauled it all back, with a stop to Tania's apartment to drop off her things. Tania took the girls home, settled them in the apartment, made sure the cable TV was working, gave them the laptop that Sanur had in storage, and got them logged on under different logins into the educational site. They went back to the orphanage to get their backpacks and the few things they owned, stopped off for food for their small refrigerator, and they were quickly settled in.

Tania realized she had no way to communicate with her new employees, so she took the teens back out to get phones for them and to get a chip for her own phone and a Thai number. Tania texted Sanur and the young ladies her new telephone number. She left them with their schoolbooks and a pile of homework and went home to her new apartment.

~

ania called home at the end of her second day to tell her friends about the new job—and new country. Corrine did a screaming thing, and both Tania and Kandace put their fingers in their ears until she finished. "We were so sad when you had to sign up for another year to pay off your school loans. This is so awesome! Show us the pool!" Tania made sure that the correct door cards were in her pocket and used her wireless headset with her cell phone. She walked around and showed her friends the apartment and the complex, then headed back to her apartment.

This time, Kandace did more than grunt. "Girlfriend, you gone and done won the lottery. We'll let you stay there, if you let us come and visit." Her girlfriends heartily approved of her Thai lifestyle, so Tania felt delighted about her decision.

Corinne spoke in a cheery voice. "Looked up the website. You'll be selling some primo stuff. But the website needs you to hammer on it."

Kandace snorted. "But your boss looks hot. Does he dye that hair?"

Tania laughed. "Probably. You're right. He's all grace and formality. Nice, actually."

"Better treat our girl right," Kandace said, and Corinne nodded. Corinne and Kandace then began pointing out what needed to be changed on the website while Tania took notes.

~

y the time Tania arrived the next morning, the floors were swept, and the girls were laughing with each other. Achara stayed, and Kannika was in her school uniform. Mrs. Amioad had spoken with the school and had gotten the girls on half school days. Tania took them both for a quick breakfast, then Kannika waved and went to school. Tania made sure that both girls had money for lunch.

Tania found Sanur in his office. "Can you take calls today while I train Achara? We'll take live ones in an hour or two."

Sanur looked up and gave Tania a quick smile while simultaneously poking at his phone and his laptop, both the latest devices. "Of course."

"Thank you so much," Tania said in her best Southern honey voice. He grinned at that.

Tania trained Achara, who listened to her every word and took notes in English and Thai with the pad and pen that Tania supplied. Tania quickly typed up some telephone scripts to use and walked Achara through them. Tania pretended to make dozens of phone calls, making Achara laugh with her ridiculous demands. Tania looked at the outgoing orders and did a series of complaint calls to Achara. "This is Achara with Kaung Import-Export for the Home. How may I help you?"

"Yes, this is Nicholas Spry. I'm calling because my tables and chairs were not delivered on time, and I'm having a party next weekend." Tania gave her voice a very dry British accent.

"I'm sorry to hear about your undelivered furniture, Mr. Spry. May I have your order number?"

"Can't remember the damn thing, can I?"

"Sir, can you spell your last name?" asked Achara. Tania complied. "Could you give me the last four digits of the credit card you used to order this?" Tania rattled off some fake numbers. "I see that your furniture is actually in Singapore and should be delivered to you by the end of the day. Is there anything else I can do for you?" Tania pretended to splutter, then hung up the pretend phone.

The girl learned script after script readily, and Tania had her go out to buy fruit for a snack. Both girls were very skinny and showed the effects of malnutrition. It was obvious they had not been receiving three meals a day. Achara readily took to having a snack break, to Tania's relief.

Tania explained the entire ordering and tracking system to Achara, as Sanur had explained it to her. Tania also had Achara scan documents, answer phones, and listen in on actual conversations that Tania had with real customers.

After lunch, Tania did the same training session with Kannika. By the end of the day, Tania was exhausted. She took the girls out for a fast street-food dinner, listened to them giggle in Thai and complain about their homework in English, and sent them up to their apartment. Mrs. Amioad arrived to ask the girls about their day, and to make sure they were doing their homework.

Tania walked home, enjoying the rapid-fire pace of life in Chiang Mai. Motorcycles roared by everywhere, there were restaurants and coffee shops on every street, and there were many food stalls to tempt her on her way home. Tania laughed to herself when she thought of the freezing winter she'd left behind, bundled up to her eyeballs.

Sanur had been polite, helpful, and perfectly willing to have Tania run the office as she saw fit. He was the best boss she'd ever had. And easy on the eyes. She laughed, fished out her first key card, and decided the pool would be the best place for her to go. Tania knew then that she was the luckiest person on the planet.

CUSTOMIZATION

Sanur used the next day's lunch hour to help Tania open a Thai bank account so she could move her money over and gave her a preloaded business credit card, taking the one he had given her back. She didn't have much, but Tania needed to keep what she had. Despite the heat and having to fill out multiple forms, Sanur was gracious and relaxed. Tania found herself relaxing too.

Things went like clockwork at work. Sanur was delighted with the new help. The young ladies were always ready to do more work, and they had schoolwork to do when things were not busy, both offline Thai and an online English course. Tania kept abreast of the online orders, made sure the warehouse for the larger items drop-shipped quickly, and arranged for pickups with individual artists all over the region. Mrs. Amioad visited every single day to be sure the girls were all right for the first week, then three or four times a week after that.

The import/export business sold fair trade craft items online from all over the region—Thailand, Vietnam, Cambodia, and some from Laos and Myanmar. The business sold tables, chairs, art pieces, carvings, sculptures, and many reusable items like straws and plates made from bamboo and other environmentally-friendly materials.

They did a brisk business with Singapore, South Korea, China,

Taiwan, Japan, and even the United States, Canada, Great Britain, and Australia. Tania's internet campaigns allowed people from all over the world to know what products were being offered, which ones were on sale or had free or reduced shipping, and what would look beautiful in someone's home. Tania sent Corinne the changes to the website, and she approved them. Sanur was delighted, especially when sales started to tick up.

$$\sim$$

Sanur met Supayalat after hours at the rooftop bar of a hotel across town. Supayalat stood and bowed. "My lord," she said in the old language. Anyone looking at them would see they were related. They had the same black hair with a copper sheen, the same formidable grace when moving, the same flat nose and whiskey eyes. She was two centimeters taller than Sanur, and had muscular arms and legs hidden by a light copper shirt and khaki pants.

"*Hteiksu.* Please, sit," said Sanur. He sat as well. They were at a table on the far side of the pool, away from both guests and other bar patrons. His investigator and right hand had chosen well. Sanur ordered a mint-lime concoction. It was not yet dinner, so he could speak freely about business. "How did you find South Korea?"

Supayalat gave him a flat stare. "Icy. I despise waste, as you know. I had the outfitters meet me at the airport. Puffy coats are...impossible." She shuddered. "I checked every place your new employee has been. All reports are very positive."

"Good." Sanur smiled and inclined his head.

Mollified, Supayalat gave the rest of her report. "The American trip was cold. And...disturbing."

"In what way?" Sanur asked. He carefully put down his drink so his glass did not make a noise.

"Her father is a criminal."

Sanur sighed. "What kind of criminal? Drugs? Guns? Tax evasion?"

"No, he attacked his own daughter."

Sanur leaned forward. "He did what?" He wasn't often surprised or shocked, but this stunned him.

"He attacked his daughter. Jake Brussell apparently intended to bed his own daughter, and she defended herself. Tania made so much noise the neighbors roused. Her mother, Rita, walked in and found him in a state of undress. Tania escaped out a window. Her father chased her, still in her nightclothes, out of the house. He had a bloody lip. A conviction, usually difficult in such cases, was swift. It was implied that there was more evidence concerning other young females." Supayalat's eyes were flat.

"She defended herself. Good," Sanur said. He realized he was clenching his jaw and both fists and strove to relax.

"Then, her mother, Rita Brussell, apparently weak of will, collapsed. She eventually took her own life."

"Such a fool to turn her back on her daughter."

"She had a son as well. Both children went to live with their father's mother, Sofia Brussell, as the mothers' parents died in a car accident years before."

"At least Tania was safe." Sanur forced himself to sip a drink he no longer wanted.

"She was in the physical sense, but her grandmother did not believe Tania or the neighbors' version of events. Sofia, the grandmother, told Tania's little brother, Sean, that his sister was to blame for destroying the family."

Sanur narrowed his eyes. "So, this young woman was attacked. Then her father went to prison and her mother committed suicide. Then her grandmother lied and told her little brother that the victim was responsible for so many tragedies. So Tania, she has no one?"

"That is where the story gets interesting. Like you with your heart-brothers, Tania went away to a small but prestigious school and made close female friends there. They met as roommates and worked together to gain scholarships and work-study programs so they could finish school more quickly. Her friends, Corinne Jackson and Kandace Walker, all stayed together for five years as roommates and heart-sisters. They all worked their way through a bachelor's degree in three years and a master's degree in a year and a half, then defended their dissertations successfully."

"Very impressive. And all three had to work the entire time?"

"Yes, but Tania and her friends were left with crushing debt. Tania came very far away from her heart-sisters and is making impressive headway. Her degree in business is helping her a great deal."

"I see," said Sanur.

"I doubted you for a moment," Supayalat admitted, bowing her head. "I see now that, as with other situations, you have keen insight into others."

Sanur gave a rueful laugh. "You mean when one of my heart-brothers and my lover stole my money?"

Supayalat bowed her head. "My lord, I must confess, I have not yet found them."

Sanur waved his hand. "I have distracted you with this matter of my new employee. Do not be too deeply concerned. In time, their money will run out. They will be forced to stop running and to begin to, as the Americans say so colorfully, run another con to get money."

"I hope it is so." Supayalat gave Sanur a slight bow. A server came by and left menus on the table. Sanur smiled. They were done talking about serious things until after dinner. "So, tell me about this place that you went to in America. Missouri? What is that place like?" Supayalat looked at Sanur balefully, and Sanur grinned.

As she spoke about heavy coats, a lack of public transportation, and cows, Sanur's mind traveled back to the past. A friend-brother he'd picked up at Thai boarding school, Somchair, had been bright enough, and considered himself good with the ladies. Sanur and Somchair went into business after the university, and the beautiful Malee soon joined them. Malee looked like a dream, moved like a breeze, and carried the delicate scent of the flower she was named after.

Sanur had been with women before, of course. His shimmery hair and aloof demeanor attracted them. He treated them gently and honorably, bought them presents, and explained that he couldn't settle down for many years, if at all. He was quiet, calm, and gentle.

Somchair was more brash, and spent a fortune on hair color, dyeing his hair a shimmery golden to match Sanur's coppery locks. Sanur did not see the jealousy in his friend's eyes. A background check showed nothing in Somchair or Malee's pasts that would hint at the betrayal to come.

The fact that Malee only had eyes for Sanur made Somchair insane. At first, Sanur kept the woman at a distance because she worked for him, and because of his friend's desire for the woman. Then Somchair came to him with an idea. "You only stay with women for a few weeks," he said. "Be with her, then let her go. She will come to me, crying, and I will be her friend."

Sanur had no intention of using the woman, so he was very clear that he would only be with her for a short time if she chose him, and that work and after-work were separate. But Sanur found himself in a trance, something that had never happened before. Weeks turned into months, then nearly a year.

Eleven months to the day after he had begun dating Malee, Sanur had woken in the morning, prepared to have flowers delivered later in the day to the office for his lady, then headed to the office. But he found the doors closed and locked, the joint account looted, and Somchair and Malee nowhere to be found.

Sanur had wept bitter tears but was delighted that they had access to only one account. He fell out of his strange lethargy, kept everything going, hired a beautiful art student to be his receptionist, and kept the business afloat. Sanur had too many people counting on him, people who needed medical care and to send their kids to school, people who could keep the lights on because of him.

The pain over being used cut deep, like a shard of metal caught in his heart, but eventually faded. The desire for revenge went much deeper. He had an excellent retainer working on it and knew the two of them couldn't hide from him—or Supayalat—forever.

Two weeks later, over a dinner of curry shrimp rice, Tania asked Sanur how they were staying in business because their profit margins were very low. Sanur laughed. "I have many investments," he explained. "Over time, many people in this region have assisted my very small, powerful family. We are in a position to help others, and this is the best way I could find to do that." He grinned. "We also keep a host of delivery people working for us. Entire families are fed based on this business."

He ate a little more rice. "What possessed you to try the orphanage? I'm not doubting the decision. The girls are extremely intelligent and very willing to do the job. But that's definitely what you Western people call 'out-of-the-box' thinking. What made you choose that route?"

"Very simple. I volunteered twice a month at orphanages in South Korea. Orphans have very few prospects. Without a family name, it's very difficult for them to get jobs. Even if the girls don't want to become receptionists in the future, their current education is paid for. And they can learn new skills as well. I plan on eventually training them in marketing. This will give them far more opportunities. Working online can help them find jobs that will allow them to go to a university."

"Thinking ahead about their futures is excellent."

Tania smiled, nodded. "Why didn't you offer me the over-office apartment?"

Sanur smiled gently. "You're a Western woman in a hot country. Why deny you the pool? Also, I figured if a Thai receptionist was hired, he or she would probably want to have that apartment."

Tania pointed out something she had noticed. "You drive a scooter the same as everyone else. Definitely no Mercedes-Benz."

Sanur laughed. "My time is too valuable to be stopped in traffic."

Tania grinned. "You also wear fine clothes, but very simple ones." She loved his simple elegant style. They both wore the slacks and professional short-sleeved shirts that everyone wore in Thailand for business. Sanur's simple wardrobe obviously cost more than Tania's.

Tania tended toward light blouses in jewel tones of blues, copper, gold, teal, and the requisite khaki or tan pants. Everything in Tania's closet matched everything else, so it took less than a minute to choose what to wear in the morning. Since Tania resembled a zombie until nearly nine in the morning, this was a good thing. Tania wore sandals or flats instead of heels, practical with the uneven sidewalks and the Thai heat.

Sanur nodded. "You must fit in where you are. Hiding in plain sight."

Tania poked at a shrimp. "Camouflage, you mean."

"Exactly. Suits in this environment just look overdone and we only wear black for funerals. It's best to be simple, classic, and ready to work hard. And, of course, take your two-hour lunches that are not common elsewhere except in the Spanish- or Italian-speaking world."

"I know some Spanish. Eighty-eight countries speak Spanish. Are you ready for me to advertise in the upper-class Spanish-speaking market? Plus, of course, there are so many people looking for an Asian vibe for their homes. I specifically targeted people of a certain age that love Asian cultures with the social media ads I created. Also, we can stage little nooks for photo shoots. Your ads are getting a little tired."

Sanur pointed at her with a chopstick. "I thought I said no business during dinner."

Tania laughed. "Give me some products to put in a photo shoot. Looks like I'm going to be training some teenage boys in how to do photoshoots for ads."

Sanur grinned at her. "The orphanage?"

"But of course."

Sanur laughed. "I approve."

"Good to know." Tania took the last of the rice. "I live for your every approving word or gesture."

Sanur threw back his head and laughed. "Seriously, despite my rule about not discussing work over dinner, I would like for you to learn the accounting so we can make reports. Sales are up, our ad campaigns are working according to the spreadsheets you insist upon sending me, and I'd like for you to understand our cash flows. My accountant does the taxation, and we have a small business lawyer on call for all of the Thai paperwork she can't handle. I would like for you to oversee the business when I am out of town. I travel frequently, looking for new things for the website."

"You could have done this from anywhere; the heart of Bangkok, Tokyo, Seoul, London, or Sydney. Why here?"

Sanur ticked the reasons off on his fingers. "First, the cost of living and conducting business are both very low here. Second, I need to be in the region to take care of all of my artisans. Third, Asia is my home. This is where I belong, where I've always belonged."

Tania sipped her fruit juice, a mint-lime iced concoction. Sanur stuck to iced mint tea. The night was sultry, the cold drinks welcome. "Must be nice to have a place like that, a home, a place to belong."

Sanur decided to take a risk. "You don't have a home back in the States?"

Tania barked out a sad laugh. "I have people that are home, close friends, but they're scattered to the winds."

"But you have a family?" he pressed.

Tania sighed. Family was all-important to Asian people, and the Thai were no exception. What to tell, what to keep back? Tired of the dance, she went with the truth. "My grandma took me in after my father attacked me one night when things went very wrong. Grandma didn't believe me about what her son did, even when my father went to prison, and my mother fell apart, eventually committing suicide. My brother sides with my grandmother."

Sanur's eyes turned stormy, but he kept his voice cool. "That sounds like a series of terrible events."

"It was. Just so you know, small-town prejudice is not a thing that can be altered or moved. Not all of it was whispers; quite a bit of it was to my face. Some of the kids at college knew, because that sort of thing is big news where I'm from. It's better to make a clean break, a new start."

Sanur nodded. "I understand new beginnings." He sighed. "I went to live with some people when my mother left. My father left a long time ago. My mother paid some people to take care of me. They lived like maharajas until the money ran out. They tired of me, for I moved like the wind or slept all day. I ended up in an orphanage."

Tania's eyes widened. "How old were you?"

"I was eleven." He took a sip of his tea. "Fear not. My majordomo found me, sent me to school that I chose from a list. I found two heart-brothers, Ketuk and Desak, at the orphanage. They joined me in boarding schools in Thailand and Australia, then the university. Like you, I received a master's in small and online businesses. Desak majored in tourism, and Ketuk in business and marketing."

"Where are they now?"

Sanur smiled. "Bali. They manage a small oceanside hotel and own some villas. I visit them from time to time."

Tania tilted her head. "I've never been there. It sounds fantastic." She waved her hand. "And this, this is heaven. It's warm, it's so green and lush, you can hear the birds sing. I spend my evenings and weekends floating in the pool and eating all kinds of delicious food. I can live so cheaply here, especially since my employer pays for my apartment." Tania grinned mischievously at him.

"I am pleased I can help." Sanur gave a slow smile that made Tania's stomach jump.

"I love the fresh fruit and vegetables here and bring them to the orphanage when I can. I teach kids how to speak, read, and write English without having to worry about a paycheck, absent co-teachers, or anyone telling me how they should be taught."

Sanur smiled gently at her. "I wondered where you were going in such a rush on Tuesday and Thursday nights."

"Now you know. Plus, I won't lie to you. I have other marketing clients. I've got to get those school loans paid off as quickly as possible. The interest is a killer."

Sanur raised his eyebrows. "I know American colleges are extremely expensive, and that most students take out loans to go." He finished off his rice. "If I may ask a deeply personal question, how much are you in debt?" He knew, of course; his investigator Supayalat had done an extensive background check on her when Sanur had received Tania's work application and resume. He knew when he met her that Tania was the person he wanted to work for him. She was obviously intelligent, a hard worker, and an expat, not a nomad moving from place to place on a whim. Her ways of thinking and her generosity had stunned him. Sanur did not want his employee going anywhere.

"I had some scholarships and grants, but they didn't cover that much. I'm in the economic hole for close to twelve thousand American dollars. That's after paying off thirty-eight percent before I got to you."

"Impressive turnaround," said Sanur. "I have a business proposition for you. The interest is killing you, correct?"

"Yes, it is." Tania ducked her head. She hated her debt with a passion.

"Why don't I give them a call?" Tania raised her eyebrows in shock. "I can see exactly how much it will take to buy out your loan. Then, I can charge you five percent interest, which is probably a much lower rate than what you are currently paying."

Tania, stunned, fought to pick her jaw up off the table. "Why would you do that?"

"Very simple. I don't want to prevent you from having other clients. But it is in my self-interest to make sure you don't have to chase clients so hard that your work suffers."

Tania narrowed her eyes at him. "I promise you, my work for you will never be compromised by my work for anyone else."

Sanur shrugged elegantly. "I know. But why take the risk? It's a simple business decision. I get an employee that wants very much for my business to grow, so that she may get a pay raise, so that she may pay me off faster. Win-win-win for everyone."

Tania narrowed her eyes at him again. "You really have that much money to throw around?"

"I have investments all over the world. And not all in tourism, which goes up and down depending on seasons. Although I do own some property here."

"Airbnb strikes again."

Sanur laughed. "Of course. I have old money, family money,

invested all over the region in a variety of currencies. I move money around to take advantage of interest rates and currency exchanges. I'm a businessman, pure and simple. I can't say every dollar, baht, or yen of my family money was completely clean in the distant past, but I can say that I run legitimate businesses. I really don't want to go to a Thai prison."

"Does anyone?" They both laughed. Tania sighed. "I agree. Thank you for your generosity." She wanted to do a happy dance but refrained. *How many investments, how much family money did this guy have? I think I'd better settle for "really rich" and leave it at that,* she thought to herself. Some of the other students at school had money, family money. But this seemed way off the scale from what she'd seen before.

Sanur waved a hand. "I already established that it is in my best interests." He grinned. "Text or email me the information tomorrow, and it will get done. I give you my word." Tania inclined her head, and he did the same back. They grinned at each other, then finished their meal.

~

*I*t took some doing, but within ten days, Sanur had bought all of Tania's debt. They worked together to set up a payment schedule to take money directly out of her paychecks, including the interest. Tania still had plenty of money to do what she wished, including seeing the sights and buying food for the orphanage. Now that she knew about his past, she wondered why he hadn't thought of hiring one of the orphans. But, then, his first receptionist apparently earned enough to go to college working for him. Maybe he was helping one person at a time. Tania snorted at herself. He was helping many people with his business. Why not hire the best? But he had taken a hell of a chance on her instead. He was still mysterious, but more approachable since Tania knew he'd been screwed over and abandoned as well.

Without the onerous interest hanging over her head, Tania

invested in some cheap Chinese tablets for the orphanage, had Wi-Fi installed there, and paid for internet services for three years in advance. She also worked with a restaurant near the orphanage to deliver cooked chicken or fish every evening for all the orphans. The kids grew rounded and happy, spoke much better English, and were able to download coursework and free educational games from the internet.

Tania helped the orphanage with its webpage, and donations began to trickle in. Tania also set up a crowdfunded donation campaign, and donations doubled within a week. Mrs. Amioad was astonished. "I cannot believe you have done so much!"

Tania laughed. "I am an internet marketer. I am so happy I had a useful skill." She tilted her head. "Their schoolwork is more important, and their English level will go up over time, but maybe I can find a low-cost Internet marketing course for those who are interested."

Mrs. Amioad laughed. "They will do anything you ask."

Tania grinned. "Nice change from some of my former students." Mrs. Amioad laughed; she knew Tania had taught elementary and middle school students in the past. Tania was a blessing; Ms. Amioad knew it with all her being.

~

Tania was delighted with her new life. She took on a few new clients to pay off her boss more quickly. Tania learned how to put together the spreadsheets that went to the accountant and changed them to track data more easily and get money to the artists more quickly.

Sanur was delighted that this time-gobbling task was taken off of his desk and showed Tania everything she needed to know about running the office in his absence. He made her a signatory on the office accounts, gave her the power to deal with customer service problems, and went away on his first trip for two weeks through Cambodia and Vietnam. Tania was stunned and touched by his faith and trust in her. She resolved to do her best. They had no major problems while Sanur was gone, and Tania was delighted when she saw an immediate increase in sales because of new ads.

~

*S*anur came back two weeks later, contracts in hand and new products in boxes on a handcart. Tania taught Kannika and Achara how to scan and file the documents and worked with new hires, Aat and Chai, on getting all of the new products photographed, onto the website, and into ads. Aat was tall and strong and was filling out due to training from lessons from a Muay Thai master Tania had paid for. Chai was smaller, quicker, and had an extremely quick mind.

Aat and Chai carried the boxes upstairs to the empty second floor and turned on the fans. "Wow!" Chai said. He pulled out a gorgeous set of carved and painted chopsticks, with jeweled wooden carvings of animals hanging from the ends.

"For...," Aat pointed at his hair.

Tania nodded. "Yes. I'll have to take the phone while you ask Kannika to put one in her hair."

Aat grinned. "Good. Now?"

"Tomorrow. We have to warn her to wear her hair up. But points for thinking of new ideas."

Chai pulled out some pillows in gorgeous brocade. "I know the right chair!" He ran to a gorgeous carved chair, set everything up, and began taking pictures.

Tania tried not to squeak when Sanur began to deliberately make noise on the last two stairs. The man was as silent as a ninja. He peered at the photo studio. "You have done a fine job here."

"These young men have learned how to make Facebook ads, from shooting to editing to posting." Aat and Chai grinned and ducked their heads at the praise. "Sanur, I would like to use company money to order some of our smaller products and have them shipped here. If we mix older and new products, we'll sell both."

"Excellent idea." Sanur came all the way up. "This will not do. I must have this enclosed and air-conditioned. It is too hot to work up here." The place was a loft, looking down on Kannika, answering phones below them. "Candles would melt up here, a pity, because we do sell candlesticks."

"I'll make the air-conditioning thing happen." Tania wiped sweat off her brow.

Sanur waved a hand. "They will charge too much. I know the right company." He pulled out his cell phone and sent a text.

Aat carefully unwrapped a glass jar and a glass lantern with a round hole cut in the top and put them on a table. "What is this?"

"The jar goes inside the lantern. You can put silk flowers or wooden dowels in there. The wood holds scent and lets the scent out slowly." Aat looked confused, and Sanur explained in liquid Thai. He found the sticks in the box. Tania assembled the jar, lantern, and sticks and put them on a small, round maroon table inlaid with silver.

"Pretty." Aat backed up, then held out his hand. Tania handed off her cell phone, and Aat knelt to get the shot.

"Excellent." Sanur looked at a new text on his phone. "The glass goes in on Thursday." He looked around. "This is...far beyond my imagining. Thank you."

"My young gentlemen like to make themselves useful." Sanur translated Tania's words, and both boys bowed, hands in prayer position to their chests. Sanur bowed back and walked soundlessly back down the spiral stairs.

Tania looked down the stairs at her boss. She knew he practiced Muay Thai. He was trim, elegant, and had lovely muscles. She grinned, sighed, and went back to work in the brain-melting heat.

It never occurred to her that her work in the gym and all the swimming toned her own muscles, and that Sanur looked at her the way she looked at him, with growing interest.

~

The glass and air-conditioning went in over the next weekend, making everyone very happy on Monday morning. Photo shoots became much more pleasant.

Their local warehouse was nearly eviscerated when the owner of some newly-built upper-class condos wanted new furnishings. They began selling furnishings to stage high-end condos, an unexpected market segment Tania began to market aggressively. Sales jumped, and the boys came on their own shifts to help keep up with the office, staging, helping Tania with the marketing as she suddenly had a lot of financial work to do, and whatever else needed to be done.

The boys began sleeping on the floor in the loft on the second story because of overcrowding at the orphanage, so Sanur had half of it converted to an actual bedroom with a wall for privacy, bunk beds, a small refrigerator, a microwave, and a rice cooker. The corner with the best light stayed the glassed-in photography studio. The boys had to share the upstairs bathroom with the girls or use the toilet downstairs, and the boys showered at the gym where they went kickboxing. Everyone was happy.

INVESTMENTS

*S*everal weeks later, Sanur took Tania out to dinner at an Indian restaurant located poolside inside a hotel. They had iced fruit drinks, tandoori chicken wraps, and quiet conversation that, for once, followed the no-business-at-dinner rule. They were both exhausted from a long week, filled with so many orders that they were beginning to have trouble keeping up. They chatted about the heat, the rain, places where they had been, keeping things light. After dinner, they took their drinks poolside and relaxed at a small table, watching hotel patrons swim back and forth.

Finally, Sanur broke his no business at dinner rule. "We need more clients, artists. So, I'm going out on another trip next week. In fact, I'm leaving tomorrow night. Some orphanages have arts programs." Sanur sipped his tea and smiled over the edge of the glass.

"Excellent," said Tania. "I'm delighted that we're doing well. I'm also very glad we hired the teens. They do the work in shifts, so no one gets exhausted. They're also plunging forward with their online work. They're very bright kids, and it's very likely they can go to an online university based in Australia, the UK, Canada, or the United States. I happen to know a lot about how to get scholarship money. I think I can get them nearly free rides if I can get them to pass high school equivalency exams."

"Ambitious. Let me know if motherhood gets to be too much." Sanur grinned.

Tania was so surprised that she slipped back into her country roots. "I ain't no mama. More like an employer, guidance counselor, teacher, mentor, and I keep the boys and the girls apart. Told all of them there's no use getting pregnant when they're this young."

Sanur threw his head back and laughed. "What do you think being the mother of a teenager actually is? I take it you gave them condoms?"

"I did. Aat's gay. He already has a boyfriend, and his own condoms."

Sanur raised his eyebrows. "That was fast."

Tania shrugged her shoulders. "They grow up fast."

"That they do." They clinked glasses and relaxed, listening to swimmers laughing in the pool's swim-up bar. Sanur watched her face, amused at her sudden motherhood. He loved Tania's agile mind and enormous heart. No doubt, he would find his business changed in some other ingenious way when he got back from his trip. She was...beautiful, inside and out. Not a coiffed, lipsticked beauty, but one with a wild heart. He had not seen her like before.

His responsibilities seemed to increase as his companies grew. It was comforting to have one business running smoothly. It was the nature of his kind to have dependents, those who would live and die based on his actions. He was recreating something that existed long ago, a system of wealth that flowed to artisans through patrons. They were not building palaces, but filling condos across the globe with beautiful things. Few people enjoyed the palaces; it was probably better this way. Pleasure multiplied. Sanur enjoyed that thought, as well as the woman with hair like flame with an agile mind in front of him.

The next day, Kannika chatted away on her headset in rapid Thai, explaining to an artist how many pieces needed to be made for a condo overlooking the beach in Da Nang, Vietnam. Aat answered an incoming call. "Sawasdee, hello, buenos dias. Kaung Import-Export for the Home, Aat speaking. How may I help you?" Despite the light rain falling on the roof, splashing into the pond in the front, Tania heard the first bit of Spanish come through Aat's headphones.

Tania raised two fingers, signaling that she would be happy to take the call. She turned away from her Facebook advertising page and rubbed her eyes. *"Buenos dias. Me llamo Tania. Como estas usted?"*

Tania had been learning more advanced Spanish from a local expat from Uruguay, a beautiful woman with long black hair and rapid-fire speech. She could chat long enough to find out what the customer needed. Tania also studied Spanish and Thai online, with the teens helping her with the Thai in exchange for her helping them study English and Spanish. All four of them complained that English was so much harder than Spanish to learn. Tania also had them learning both languages through free YouTube videos. They loved learning through songs and movies.

Their last photo shoot against cardboard walls painted sunny yellow and a bright cobalt blue had garnered a lot of Spanish speakers looking to decorate. Tania took a sizable order, totaling to nearly two thousand American dollars, based on villa pictures that the Spaniard had sent in a link to her.

Senor Padilla sounded very happy when Tania gave him many suggestions to help him decorate his villa. Tania had just hung up the phone when another Spanish-speaking call came through. Tania sighed, realizing that she wouldn't be able to create more Facebook ads until after lunch.

They kept the phones open for lunch by eating in shifts. Tania had a yearning for really good pad thai, so she walked over another block, sat down on a bright red stool, and watched the wizened old woman make the pad thai in a skillet, her arms moving like blurs stirring the dish, adding spices, lime juice, and peanuts at the end. The spices made Tania drool.

The rain had stopped, and the day was hot and muggy. What seemed like a thousand scooters and motorcycles zipped by, with the occasional car. It was far easier and cheaper to drive a motorcycle in Thailand, filling up was only a few dollars a month. People dressed for the heat, in light clothes. The sounds of Thai, English, Tagalog, and German fill the air, with the occasional Vietnamese and Indonesian thrown in. People gesticulated at each other and bought food from street vendors. Backpackers walked by with their red, blue, or black backpacks on their backs, poking at the maps on their cell phones. Digital nomads walked by, computers slung over their shoulders in backpacks and shoulder bags, on their way to Nimman, the section of the city where they liked to congregate and share work spaces and coffee shops.

It was a wild, loud bustle, so different from the hills and hollers where Tania had grown up. She loved every minute on the street, the passers-by fun to watch as she ate.

Tania missed Sanur, his quiet presence at his desk, their lunches and dinners. It was strange; he was her boss, yet he was becoming a friend. He had a presence. A gravity. When he entered a room, everyone paid attention to him. There was a formality to his speech and movements missing in modern society. He was fascinating, and mysterious. He had no Facebook, Twitter, Instagram, or other social media accounts. No personal website. He was a blank.

She rushed back to work and stayed busy. People love free things, and they included small free items in each packet such as chopsticks or tiny statuettes. Coordinating items from all over the world was much easier than it would have been in the past because Sanur had set up drop-shipping warehouses in Prague, Panama City, and Buenos Aires. They kept their bestselling items there, greatly decreasing shipping times.

They were so busy that Tania literally could not hear herself think for the rest of the day. She went back to the same street vendor for dinner, watched the young people close out the office and go laughing in a knot to find food before settling down in a coffee shop with homework.

Despite her exhaustion, Tania knew she needed to let off some steam. She went home, changed into her tankini, lifted some weights, worked out on the elliptical machine, and headed for the pool. Tania swam until she couldn't lift her arms, went upstairs, showered, and dressed for a night out.

She found herself in a little club called Dancing Breeze, ordered a lime slush, then danced to calypso music. Tania stayed on the edge of the crowd, as most of them were paired off. Some of them were dancing rather dirty. Tania smiled with amusement. She realized that sex was something that could not be ignored, and at some point she'd have to get back into dating. Maybe her mysterious boss? She shook her head, startled at the thought. But right now the heat, music, and sweaty bodies was enough, just for tonight.

Tania ended up dancing with a group of young women that were getting slowly sloshed, an Argentinian, a German, a Kazakh, two Russians, and a Brit. She got the story from them in between sets. They had met on a tour van and have become fast friends on a wild tour of Southeast Asia. Tania took in their stories. Most of them were just out of college or in the middle of their last year. Two were digitally employed, living and working in Southeast Asia to save money.

Tania knew there were so many digital nomads living in Thailand that part of the economy was devoted to the shared workspaces, coffee shops, and low-rent housing that they enjoyed. Some were successful, some weren't. Tania admired their driving ambition, but most of them weren't savvy enough to truly make a go of it. Tania knew from experience that hard work didn't necessarily make a dent in the real world.

But this was not the night for rough-and-tumble musings. This was the night for dancing, lime slushies, laughter, and the occasional sloe-eyed gaze from across the room. It was either that or insanity. Tania chose dancing over losing her mind. She pretended her boss, with his smile and urbane manners, would stop and dance with her at any minute. He was hot, and she was very much alive, in paradise.

~

Tania didn't get out of bed until nearly noon the next day, which was strange for her. Late nights just weren't her thing, not anymore. She wondered if her grandmother had rubbed off on her, waking up at the crack of dawn, rooster or no rooster. Her grandmother didn't raise them; they were actually nearby. So were fat sheep that became slim after shearing again in the spring, the lambs dancing in the spring sunlight, free to move without their winter coats. The endless acres of cows, chewing their cud under trees, the trees bending with the wind across the fields.

Tania had come a long way and she knew it, but she still looked back in her mind, primarily with her stomach. What she wanted was sage sausage in the morning, orange chicken for lunch, and hot biscuits with honey and a good ham steak for dinner. She didn't miss America, not really. She did miss the horses running across the field, foals running with their mothers, spindly legs stretching out for the first time. And, of course, the food.

Tania stretched, laughing, when she remembered selling candy for a school trip in a late April snowstorm, making people feel so sorry for her in her bedraggled state that she came in third in the entire school in candy sales. She laughed at herself, realizing she had actually been an entrepreneur from an early age.

You've come a long way baby, she thought to herself. *Rise and shine.* She got up, rolled out a yoga mat, and began her stretches. She followed with meditation, a short ten-minute app that cleared her head for the day. She desperately needed it, considering how busy her life was. And because of all her strange thoughts about her hot boss.

After breakfast, Tania went to a temple and did some meditation. She lit a stick of incense, letting the smoke rise to the sky. She put her sandals back on and walked around some more. She went back home to change out of her sweaty T-shirt and shorts and dressed in light blue shorts and a dark blue top with a feather emblazoned across the top and all the way around the side in red and gold.

Tania wandered so far that she ended up at a taco restaurant about three kilometers away from her apartment a bit early. She sat down, ordered a lime slush, and munched her way through chips and salsa while waiting for Sanur to arrive.

He found her in the back of the restaurant with his eyes, waved, and walked in that strange, sinuous way that he had, dodging servers and drunken tourists as if they surrounded him all the time. Tania wondered if he had been a boxer or a dancer in a past life, for he moved with such grace. His black hair with its coppery sheen shone in the light, brushing his collar. He had on a short-sleeved copper shirt and khaki slacks. His eyes looked tired from his journey.

The server, a Thai girl in the requisite heels, short dress, and huge crimson smile came by to take their order. Tania ordered a chimichanga, and Sanur ordered a taco combo. Both ordered iced tea. "How was your trip?" asked Tania.

"Long. I know Southeast Asia the best. I can find the poorest of the poor, the people with great talent and no money to realize their dreams." He smiled. "Just like the orphans you hired. Highly intelligent, driven, ready to work. Insanely grateful that the rent is paid for, and that they have money for food, medicine, and anything else they need. Eager to learn new skills and humbly seeking any chance they can get. They won't find anything as good as what we are willing to give them."

"There is a we now? Last I checked, I don't own any percentage of the business."

Sanur raised his eyebrows. "Is that what you want?"

Tania grinned. That hadn't been directly on her mind, but now that he brought it up, why not? "Two percent of the gross," she offered. "Hell of an incentive for me to keep growing the business."

Sanur laughed. "You Americans, always willing to...What do you say? Drive a hard bargain."

"I've seen you drive a hard bargain or two. Don't go pretending you're all sweetness and light."

Sanur laughed so hard he nearly dropped his tortilla chip with its load of mango salsa. "Sweetness and light? Far from it. I'm a creature of the dark. I'm not happy about staying up during the day." He narrowed his eyes at her. "Now that we're dealing with the other side of the world, I can take the night shift. Do you think the young ones are good enough to run the store during the early morning hours?"

"They definitely are. It doesn't really matter when I do the Facebook ads. I can check that anytime, day or night. Same with keeping up with the accounting, and the Spanish speakers primarily call later in the day. They can always transfer the call to me if they run into a Spanish speaker."

"What about you? Are you a morning person?" Sanur asked, a gleam in his eyes.

"Used to be. Started out in a suburb, big houses and trees, a nice girl with a little brother to help take care of. We rode bikes everywhere. We had a piano, but I went rebel and chose the guitar."

"Then things changed." Sanur understood. Things had changed suddenly for him as well.

Tania shrugged. "I went to live with my grandma. Ended up in a holler, that's a little valley, in between two big farms. Surrounded by sheep, cows, a few goats to keep down the kudzu. Kudzu is vegetation, an ivy, that's almost impossible to kill. Grandma was up at the crack of dawn, even before the roosters woke everyone else up. I promised myself I'd never be poor again, and if that means getting up at the crack of dawn, that's what I'll do."

"Try it two days a week."

"Try what?"

"Evenings. Isn't that when most of the Spanish-speaking people call?"

"Yes, it is. Swing shift where I'm from is usually one p.m. to nine p.m. That sound good to you?"

"You run my business. You decide."

"I love choosing my own hours!" Tania grinned as the food arrived.

"You do everything my former business partner did." Sanur bit into a chicken taco.

"Former business partner? Did he move away?"

Sanur choked, drank down some iced tea with mint. "You could say that. He cleaned out the account he had access to, worth about half a million American dollars, and took my girlfriend, who used to be my administrative assistant, with him."

Tania whistled and mimed stabbing Sanur in the heart. Sanur grimaced. "We are not biologically related, but I considered him to be a brother."

"Not anymore."

"Not anymore." Sanur sipped his drink.

"You need to get your money back. My daddy stole my childhood. My mama abandoned me in the worst way possible. The last two people left of my family didn't believe any of the words coming out of my mouth, which stole my trust." She leaned forward, her eyes blazing. "People that steal keep stealing. You've got to put a stop to them, or they'll keep doing it. He took your money, he took your girl." She narrowed her eyes at him. "Sorry to say this, but you're better off without the girl. But the money, the money you need back."

"Agreed. He's good at hiding, I'll give him that. I sent someone after him who can find anything and anyone. She says she's making progress, and she's getting much closer. I don't think he'll be able to escape for very much longer."

"You hired a shark?" asked Tania.

"More like a snake." Sanur smiled sardonically. "Malee, my ex-girlfriend, is smart, ruthless, and better than Somchair at nearly everything. My retainer will find them and make them pay. They deserve each other. In fact, it's likely that she took the money from him, and he no longer has it." Sanur ate another taco.

"She's a con artist," realized Tania. "I used to know them girls. Pretty, vivacious, made you want to give them the shirt off your back. But that was never good enough for them. They wanted to do as little as possible to get the most they could, in any way they could, no matter how illegal or cruel. Hate them bitches."

Sanur was impressed. "Your accent becomes more and more Southern the more angry you get. Don't be angry." He touched her hand. "I'm already getting even."

"Good." Tania was sad when Sanur withdrew his hand. She decided to change the subject. "So do I get my two percent or not?"

Sanur laughed. "You just want to be able to pay me back more quickly."

"Damn straight." Tania laughed. "Besides, yes, you can probably find someone other than me to run your business. But I have really good ideas, and sales are up close to forty percent. I found an entirely new market for you, and you didn't even have to hire an extra Spanish-speaking person to deal with the overflow."

"We should do that. Your strength isn't speaking Spanish, or even customer service. You make our business grow, and that's what we need." Sanur ran his hands through his shoulder-length hair, making the bits on top stand up straight. "There are families that are relying on us to eat. Many are single parents. Many have sick children or parents. Most of them live in the worst slums you can possibly think of. I'm talking sewage in the front yard, or a house made up of a few pieces of metal or wood."

Tania could see it in her mind. It wasn't a pretty picture. She nodded grimly. Sanur raised a hand, moved it outward. "Now they have food, clothing, medicine, can take their parents and children to the hospital, can move out of the slums. They have supplies for their art, and even hire those around them to help. A single person in a slum getting money, moving out, taking their families and friends with them, can have an enormous impact on so many different people."

"I get it. This is all through hard work, the work they do to make what we sell, the work we do to sell it. Our job is making people happy all over the planet on both sides, the artists and the clients."

Sanur grinned. "Yes, you do understand."

"Tell me about just one of them." Tania sipped her drink, the icy lime-tea goodness welcome on her parched throat.

Sanur smiled, pleased at Tania's interest in the artists. "One woman lives on the coast of Cambodia. She collects seashells and driftwood. She makes those beautiful ocean objects we sell. Jewelry, picture frames. Her eleven-year-old son carves statues from driftwood. Her daughter helps her collect seashells. Now both her kids go to school, they have health care, they are happy and healthy. The son taught his mother how to replicate the best pieces, so he has time to do his school work."

"I know these driftwood statues. They're selling like crazy in Spain. They're so whimsical, humorous. So much fun." She smiled. "Think I'm going to order one for my desk. And probably some of the necklaces."

"We're also going to need to find a Portuguese speaker. I've noticed we have some sales from there."

"The two I talk to speak perfect English. It's going to cost us money to have some Spanish- and Portuguese-speaking people ready to answer questions, but we could do it virtually."

"They can always contact us when they really don't understand something. It's more cost-effective to do it that way than it is to hire many different native speakers."

"Wait a minute." Tania sat up straight. "We're surrounded by digital nomads from every country on the planet. We just have to hire a few of the right ones to answer questions. They can always transfer the call to us if they are completely confused. The non-American ones usually speak several different languages."

"Three percent. And that's my final offer."

Tania grinned, and sipped her ice lime drink. "Glad to see I'm wearing you down." Sanur gave her a slow smile that curled her toes. "Besides, that goes to paying off the money I owe you."

"It does. Think of all the delicious interest I'm losing out on by increasing your pay." He smirked, an expression so different from his calm urbanity that Tania had to choke down a laugh.

"My heart bleeds for you."

Sanur snorted. "So, any other ideas to improve the bottom line?"

"Nothing more for my to-do list." Tania rolled her eyes.

Sanur laughed, his teeth blindingly white against his dusky skin. "You should see mine."

"My job is to take as much off your plate as I can. That leaves you time to find more for us to sell, new things that will intrigue buyers. We can't afford to get stale."

"Your job is to sell and to run the office. Most of the time, that's two separate jobs."

"The quad helps me with the online ads."

"The quad? Oh, our four Thai teens." Sanur looked Tania right in the eyes, his chocolate brown eyes boring into her hazel ones. "We can't get too big. The whole point is for these to be one-of-a-kind things, and if we spend too much on overhead, the artist won't get much anymore."

"So, double in size and stop?"

"Something like that."

"Keep it lean, agile."

"Like you." Sanur gave her a slow smile.

"Like me." Tania raised her eyebrows.

"No more business. Let's dance." Sanur paid the bill and took her to the small dance floor. Sanur put one hand on her waist, then the other. She put her hands on his shoulders and moved to the music. Tania had been taking salsa lessons and a little merengue. So, she was able to follow his lead and found herself laughing and whirling. His paper-and-incense smell clung to her. His hands on her felt warm, inviting. He looked young, like a very classy international party man in his early thirties without all the drinking and dissipation.

The band started playing a song with a more calypso beat, and she moved. Sanur wound around her, back and forth, winding closer and farther away, making her laugh. It was better than any late-night drinking fantasy had been.

There was pulsing heat, a pounding beat, sheets of rain outside the open doorway, and a flow she'd never felt before. Tania felt part of it all, the rain, the hot wind, the beat of the music. She felt herself getting closer and closer to Sanur. Then, he ordered her another drink. They cooled down, laughing, and he called a *tuk tuk* to take them home.

He dropped her off at her door, entwined his hands in hers, and kissed both her cheeks gently. She smiled up at him and sighed when he turned and walked away. She wanted...more. A lot more.

ROCK GODDESS

$\mathcal{A}$ week after the Africa trip, Tania and Sanur had another no-business-rule dinner. Lupe was off with friends that she collected like bracelets, mostly digital nomads. They liked to run around the Nimman District together. The quad, now six since they had hired Daw and Kasem from the orphanage, were busy with their studies. Daw was slight but classically handsome, and Kasem was small for his age, but so energetic it was hard keeping up with him.

Sanur was still exhausted from his trip across a giant continent, and Tania was elated because she had created an initiative from scratch with the African clients that was selling very well. She was getting close to seventy percent done with paying off her largest loan and was absolutely thrilled to take a night off. They shared garlic naan bread and butter chicken with cold mint *lassi*, a yogurt drink.

Sanur stared at his food. "I can't decide whether or not I'm too tired to eat. I had to open bank accounts in numerous cities, set up micropayments for cell phones, deliver cell phones, bicycles, or motorcycles to those who needed them, and spend some time on hiring someone to drill for fresh water for some of the smaller villages. My other company paid for English training in schools for countries that didn't have English as its primary language. Nigeria does, and it was a pleasure going through there." He paused to eat more garlic naan bread.

"That's excellent." Tania was amused by Sanur's enthusiasm, and that he was inadvertently breaking his own no business during dinner rule.

"They were all very surprised that a Thai-based company was willing to invest so much into local infrastructure and economies. I had to explain that artists work best when their children are in school, they can communicate with me via cell phones to be sure their products get to market, and that they work much better when they have water and electric power that they can afford." Sanur remembered he had food in his hand and used his naan bread to scoop up some chicken.

"Were you able to contact any orphanages?"

"Some of the collectives were already working with them. I encouraged that, making sure those young people have jobs they can step into and can afford an education." Sanur tore off more naan bread and grabbed some chicken with it before popping it in his mouth.

"That's fantastic. The kids in my older class are doing so well that they're teaching the younger ones with me, and they're having a lot of fun making videos and podcasts for their school." Tania went for the chicken before Sanur ate it all.

"You work hard and volunteer even harder," observed Sanur. "You need to take more time off."

"That's why I volunteer during the week and not on weekends," said Tania. Sanur smiled. This woman educated the powerless, the hallmark of his clan. His admiration for her was growing. "I work earlier on orphanage days and take time to go work with them after school, food, and chores. They are wonderful, so ready to learn. As you know, I hired two more orphans to work."

Tania had told designers and other high-value customers who were slowly being converted into friends about the orphans and the online crowdfunding page. The orphanage got a lot more funding, and slowly, one by one, then in twos or threes, the orphans were being adopted by Thai people, as well as by visiting overseas teachers, entrepreneurs, and other expats from various countries.

"It's going to get hot in there. Are you trying to cook the children?"

Tania made a face at him. "All of the office is now air-conditioned, so they won't fall over during the hot months."

Sanur grimaced at her. "I thought we agreed not to talk directly about work during dinner." He washed the butter chicken down with some *lassi*.

Tania put her hands up in the air, conceding the point. "I promise."

They devoured the rest of their chicken, washed up, and went for a walk. The streets were slick with rain, though the clouds had blown away. Neon reflected off the black pavement. They argued about whether to see a movie or go dancing. Dancing won.

Tania loved the feel of the street, the pulse-pounding music streaming out from shops, bars, and clubs. It was a Friday night, and many shops were still open. Tania squealed and walked into a store selling helmets, leather, and Harley gear, making Sanur laugh. She found the helmet she liked and bought it. "You don't have a scooter or a scooter license yet," pointed out Sanur.

"Both my motorcycle and driver's licenses are still good from the US, and I obtained universal licenses for both in South Korea," Tania informed Sanur with an arched eyebrow.

Sanur held up his hands, palms out, in mock surrender. Tania went to the next store and tried on, then bought, a flared skirt that barely covered her hips and thighs in black covered with silvery chains and buckles. She also bought a T-shirt of a skeleton wearing a red bandana on a motorcycle. She put the entire outfit on, squealed, then came out of the changing room with her old clothes in a bag.

Sanur was stunned to see her beauty. Here in the land of year-round warmth, a pool and workout center in her apartment complex, and her increasingly strenuous workouts, she had lost several kilos. Then, she'd gained it back in muscle. This had given her pleasing curves. So, when Tania's hips swayed to the driving rock beat in the store, it drove Sanur a little mad.

The life his Tania—When had she become *his Tania?*—had lived before coming to Asia had been so different from his own. Sanur wondered what goddess he managed to please to have a woman like Tania in his life. Her English would change from proper to the back roads where she grew up, her eyes would darken, and she would entrance him with something unexpected. The woman who stood before him, dancing to the shop's blaring rock music in her new clothes, was nothing like Malee.

Tania had a massive and generous heart to match her intelligence. This American expat had been through several nightmares already and was determined not to go back there. She had friends who loved her, and she only asked for what she deserved. She paid her bills and her debts, worked hard, and gave back to the community around her from the second day after they had met.

Tania also had a special gift, the ability to see inside people, to see the potential. She could do it with art but worked magic with people. Her perceptive eyes were worth more than he could ever say.

Sanur didn't know if he could give up his heart again, or if he even had one after everything he'd been through. But he wanted to try. This woman had a zest for life that made him want to live, a way of seeing things that made him want to change his perceptions. He had never wanted to change himself for anyone before, but she made him want to grow, to shed his old ways like a skin and embrace new ones. All of these things were valued by his people, and he was not a stupid man. But how does one hold on to glitter floating in the wind?

"I know a place we can go," he said, diverting Tania from the task of buying all the silver rings, necklaces, and pairs of earrings in the store. She wore her new purchases, laughing. He walked her back to his bike, and she laughed as she put on her new helmet. He put her old clothes under the seat and drove her to the only hard rock club he knew. It was called Spike Devil, and it was in the heart of the Nimman District.

She made him stop nearby so she could go into a beauty store and get some deep purple lip gloss. She put it on after paying for it, and kissed him lightly, so quickly it might not have happened at all. She tasted like dark berries. He felt his heart unbend, his icy calm flow out the window. It felt...wild. Amazing. Like lightning striking a tree.

He paid the cover, and they went in as the band was playing Def Leppard's "Armageddon It." Sanur had never tried to dance to hard rock music in his life, but he found her gyrating into him appealing. He was soon covered with sweat, but didn't care, pounding out the beat on one thigh with his left hand. His right hand was on her hip, and she moved into him. Sanur moved like a snake, sinuous and curving, making her go wild.

The lead singer stepped back in the middle of "Love Bites," choking, gesturing for water, while the band continued to play. Sanur was stunned when Tania ran up to the stage, hopped up, whispered something to the band, grabbed the mic from the lead singer, and the band went into the opening riffs of Guns 'N Roses' "Sweet Child of Mine." Tania sang the song in a growly voice that made everyone in the club dance, and made Sanur stand there like a fish, his mouth wide open. Tania hit the notes perfectly, holding them, screaming them out into the audience.

The band's singer was still onstage off on the side, recovering his breath, and he took off his shirt, making the crowd scream. By the time they got to the coda, the Thai singer with the wild black hair was ready to roar. He stole the mic from the guitarist, and Tania and the singer stalked each other across the stage. They sang the lines back and forth to each other, making the crowd go wild.

More and more people crushed into the club, attracted by the music, and Sanur found a nice, safe wall to lean against. They did the final growly notes, and the band, Rose Guns, obviously a tribute band, reveled in the adulation of the crowd. Tania grinned, and went into a growly-screaming rendition of "You Should Be Mine" with the lead singer. She was a maniac on the stage, taking turns singing with the drummer, guitarist, and the lead singer.

Tania sang an extremely dirty "Rocket Queen" that had Sanur wondering why he was holding back with this woman. Why did his aloofness still wrap around him? Could it not be cast aside for this magical woman? Any thoughts of his mistakes with Malee seemed remote, like they happened to someone else. They sang "Welcome to the Jungle" and "Paradise City," and had the crowd screaming the lyrics with them. They ended the set with a very stripped down "Patience," and the entire audience sang the final coda with them.

Sanur went up to Tania, climbed up on stage, and in the heat of the moment, gave her the kiss he wanted to give her while she was singing "Rocket Queen." The crowd went wild. Tania looked at Sanur, stunned. Sanur, terrified that he had gone much too far, put his lips next to her ear and said, "I have to go. You stay here and enjoy your night."

Sanur held up his phone as if someone had called him and jumped off the stage. Somehow, he moved his legs, pushed past the sweating horde, slid out, got on his bike, and turned it on with sweaty, fumbling fingers. His heart pounded, his brain screamed, and he rode out into the night, trying to catch his breath.

Tania wondered who the hell was calling her boss in the middle of the night, but she decided she was too busy to figure it out. She still felt the heat of the kiss on her lips, stunned by its intensity. She felt drunk, high on being with a band again. As a teen, school bands had gotten Tania out of the house, and she could play guitar and drums. The drums allowed her to beat out her feelings. The guitar allowed her to create a rhythm where there wasn't one. Rock was the best musical genre ever because she could be as loud and angry as she wanted.

The band completed the set, and the drummer pulled her backstage. They ended up in a tiny room painted blue, and the drummer silently handed Tania a bottle of water. They drank in silence for a minute, catching their breath. "I'm Rangi," said the drummer guy. "Axel here is our singer, Nim, the guitarist, Flix on bass, and I'm on drums." They were a mix of Thai and Western people. The lead singer and guitarist were Thai, Flix was an Aussie, and Rangi a Maori Kiwi.

Axel was tall and skinny like his namesake in his heyday, with hair that sprung from his head and went all the way down the shoulders, black with streaks of gray and blue. Flix was also reed-thin, and it looked as if his bass was too big for him. His hair was brown with blond streaks from surfing, and he had a deep surfer's tan. Rangi was a big man with a deep chest, a throaty growl for a voice. He was constantly pounding out a beat on his leg, his arm, a table, a chair. He seemed to be in a contest with himself to come up with more complicated beats. "We need a sheila," said Flix. "You'll do."

"Give her some of your hair stuff, Axel," said Rangi.

"Girl needs boots," said Nim. "Those sandals won't last long."

"I'll take care of it," said Axel. He dragged her out the door and down the alley. There was a shop selling boots open in the middle of the night, and Tania went ahead and got the damn boots. They were low, sexy black boots, and she bought thin black socks before sliding into them. They were a quarter of the price she would have paid in the States.

Then Axel dragged her out and back to the club, back to the tiny room with a golden star on the door where the band members were pouring drinks down their throats. Axel had makeup and pots of bright color; blue, purple, silver, green, and a shocking orange. "Pick your poison," he said. "It's wax, washes right out, in case you have a day job." She pointed to the pots of blue and silver, and Axel stared at her for a long moment. "Ends or scalp? That red of yours is gorgeous."

"Twists, baby," said Nim.

"Okay, I'm stupid," said Axel. "Drink this." He twisted the lid off another cold bottle of water and thrust it into her hand. Tania did as Axel demanded, draining the bottle. Axel took out strips of her hair, and started alternating with blue with this left hand, and silver with his right. Within minutes she looked like a rock goddess. Axel washed his hands, then applied spray glitter to her hair, washed his hands again, then did her eyes with heavy eyeliner in black, her lids in copper and silver. He made up her lips with bright crimson. "I'm still the best," Axel said.

Rangi went over the set list. "I think we should do 'Love Bites,' along with 'Pour Some Sugar on Me.'"

"Too slow, man," said Flix.

Tania withdrew a wad of Thai *baht* from her bra. "Somebody buy me a bottle of champagne." At their flat stares, she said, "You know. 'Pour Some Sugar on Me'?"

"I like this sheila," said Flix. "Your name is Tina, No, Toni. No, Josie."

"I like Josie," said Rangi. Someone pounded on the door, and Rangi said, "We're on. Axel, you better be done with her. Josie, come with us."

So Tania became a Josie, learned to strut in low-heeled boots all over the stage, and rocked Def Leppard's "Pour Some Sugar on Me" when she shook up the champagne bottle, popped the champagne cork into the air, and sprayed the champagne all over the crowd, to howls of laughter and cheers. She passed the bottle to the crowd who passed it around. Then Tania strutted her stuff and sang the dirtiest "Rocket Queen" anyone had ever heard.

NO EXPLANATION

Tania didn't get out of the club until after three in the morning. The *tuk tuk* driver dropped her off at home, and she slept for nearly eleven hours straight. She woke up thirsty and hoarse, with a pounding headache and smears of colored hair gunk on the pillow. The sun streaming in the windows made her clench her eyes closed.

Tania drank half a liter of water along with some naproxen sodium to get rid of the headache, showered, and did a load of sheets with the hair gunk-striped pillow case. She managed to keep down an English muffin, then a mango. She stretched her tired muscles, popped her neck, read a science fiction book, and watched a movie.

When her headache faded along with her roiling stomach, she went out to the street to get some noodles. Stomach settled and hunger abated, she washed up at home and brushed her teeth, put on her tankini, and floated in the pool.

Sanur hadn't left a single message to explain why he ran out so quickly the night before—with her old clothes and her new helmet in his bike's under-seat storage. Tania hoped everything was all right and assumed he would have told her if something had gone wrong with the business. *He's your boss. He doesn't owe you an explanation*, she said to herself, over and over. But she still wanted one. Wait, she had kissed him first. Just a peck. Something that she had been wanting to do for a long time. Did *she* sexually harass *him*? What had she been thinking?

She got a hold of Corinne first, who then brought Kandace in. Kandace and Corinne wanted to know all of the gory details. "Oh my god, you're a rock goddess!" raved Kandace. "Pictures! Must send pictures!"

"Video," said Corrine. "Are you, like, going to be on the band's website? And what the hell is the name of the band?"

"Rose Guns," said Tania, somehow finding the words in her brain. "They're basically a Guns 'N Roses tribute band. They play in the only hard rock club I'm aware of in Chiang Mai." She poured more water down her throat. She definitely felt dehydrated.

"You didn't do 'Rocket Queen,' did you?" asked Corrine.

"She did," said Kandace. "Do it. Do it for us."

"Do it," said Corrine.

"You females is beyotches." Tania cleared her throat, drank some water, and sang a breathy, filthy rendition of "Rocket Queen." Her two best friends clapped, then Tania said, "I bought a bottle of champagne and poured it on the crowd during the Def Leppard song, 'Pour Some Sugar on Me.'"

"You are so dirty. Tell Mama Kandace." Tania sighed, and gave a blow-by-blow explanation of everything that happened the night before. When she got to the kiss, Corinne and Kandace both stopped her. "What the fuck?" asked Kandace. "And no text today, no phone call, nothing explaining what the fuck happened? Either that's a real emergency, or your boss is a dick. Or he thinks with his dick."

"I think it's a combination of sexual harassment and cold feet," said Corrine. "He thought, hey, don't want a lawsuit, think I'll run away really quickly."

"He still being a dick," opined Kandace.

"I don't know what to do. I had no idea what to do or say last night because the man is hot as hell. That kiss made my hair catch on fire.

Not literally." Kandace and Corinne laughed. "What do you say at a time like that? Hey, that was kind of cool, my hair just caught on fire?"

Corinne let out a belly laugh. "It's a start."

"And now he's pulling a disappearing act. Did he suddenly hate it?" asked Tania.

"Did he hear you do 'Rocket Queen'?" asked Kandace.

"Yes," said Tania, in a really small voice.

"Possibly the heat of the moment," said Corinne, and hummed the song with the same name, making Tania laugh. "He may have scared the hell out of himself."

"Or you're so hot he swooned and couldn't handle it," said Kandace.

"The man has the grace of a cat and is so cool that he has several million-dollar bank accounts and doesn't fly first class." Tania grimaced, drank more water.

"I would fly first class, if I had that kind of money," said Kandace, affronted.

"Business class is good enough, and much better for the price," said Corrine. "So, he's tight with his money. But you said he's paying you part of the gross? That's pretty weird for someone like you just starting out in this particular business, isn't it? It says he really trust you. And he goes out of town all the time and leaves you running the business, trusts you to hire people, do the accounts."

"And, you said some jackoff stole his money and his girl," said Kandace. "So he trusted you after he already got screwed over. That shows he has some damn character, that he sees you for who you really are. Even though he hasn't known you long, he knew you could do it and that you are trustworthy. So no, I don't think he hates it. I think he got overwhelmed or scared, maybe about the whole sexual harassment thing, and then zipped off before he could do something stupid."

"If that's true, I should go into the office on Monday and act as if nothing has happened at all. He may be too embarrassed, or he may be really sickening and apologize." Tania sighed.

"So sickening," said Kandace, dryly.

Tania's phone dinged. "Hold on, ladies. Unknown number. Hello?" Tania listened for a while. "Yeah, I don't know the place, but that's what *tuk tuk* drivers are for. So, two blocks away from the department store? Okay, but I'm going to need sustenance before I do this thing. Yeah sure, food court sounds good. Probably take me twenty. See ya."

Tania hung up, ignored her friends on the computer screen, ran over to her closet, put on a camisole with a shelf bra, and started layering blue and silver tank tops over it. She put on her skirt from last night and her boots, and said, "Meeting the band. Forgot I gave Flix my digits. What do you think?"

"Not trampy enough," said Kandace. "Go ruffle the hell out of your hair, put on all the jewelry you own except the pearls, and I'll walk you through the makeup. I'll have you looking like a rocket queen in no time."

~

*T*ania was about five minutes late, but successfully found the food court. The secret was to go into the mall, stay on the first floor, and go to the back to the food court the locals use. The food there was usually dirt cheap, and as good as anything else, unless you were craving Western food. She ordered the cheapest but best pad thai.

"Was going to rag on you for being late," said Rangi. "But I see it was a good idea. Forgot that girls take longer to get ready."

"Sit," said Flix, pointing to an empty chair. "The bar owner loves us, specifically you. Said he sold six bottles of champagne after your little trick onstage. Sheer genius."

"We packed them in," said Axel. "I've never seen that many people in that room at the same time, even during high season."

"Tourist season," translated Flix. "Eat up, Josie, we've got to practice a new set list."

Tania rolled with having a new name. "Do you guys know any Lita Ford?" Tania wolfed down some pad thai. "And 'Dead or Alive' would be awesome."

"Are there any '80s bands you don't know?" asked Rangi.

Tania shrugged. "I was angry. You can bang drums and make a guitar scream with '80s music."

"As long as you don't sing Alanis Morissette. That woman was fecking angry," observed Rangi.

Tania got a demonic look on her face and growled the first few bars of "You Oughta Know" into her straw. She grinned, and said, "Who can sing Ozzy Osbourne? Real slow," she amended.

"Got to pull up the songs on your cell phone," observed Flix.

"Got it," said Rangi. He pulled up the lyrics and showed them to Axel, and Axel started humming, recognizing the haunting and rather disturbing rock ballad between Lita Ford and Ozzy Osbourne entitled "Close My Eyes Forever." Tania sang the line about licking blood from her blade, and Rangi grimaced. "Not at the table, luv," he said, making everyone laugh.

The practice room building close to the bar was low and squat and painted a particularly ugly shade of puce, the space specifically put aside for musicians. It had sound baffling, and a little recording studio in the back for those who wanted to pay the money. The walls were black, the purple lighting mysterious. They all put in a few *baht* for the room. Violinists and singers practiced in other rooms; they could see them through the tiny panes of glass in the doors.

Axel had to baby his voice because he had cracked it the night before. Tania pulled up a song list. "Don't think you should sing 'Dead or Alive,' 'Sweet Emotion' is better. Won't make your voice crack." They ran through all of the Guns 'N Roses songs first, just one verse and the chorus.

Tania put all of the musicians on a sheet music streaming service with a ten-songs-a-month program, popular with bands and musicians. They got through the Lita Ford just fine, to her surprise. They had fun with Def Leppard, laughing as Tania tried to make herself more and more slutty with her dancing while singing.

They went ahead and practiced "Dead or Alive" and "Close My Eyes Forever." Axel and Tania figured out how to trade off lines and stanzas and developed a system of signals to determine who sang next, and how Tania could cover Axel if he forgot the words.

They had a hefty dinner at a Chinese place down the street after practice, sharing dishes, and they went towards the bar with their instruments.

Tania took a side trip to a store filled with musical instruments. Rangi stayed with her while the rest of them went to the bar to be sure everything was set up correctly. It was crazy, but Tania knew she was at seventy-two percent through paying off her bills and projected to have all of them gone soon because of the new product line. So she splurged. She picked out a metallic blue electric guitar, a small amp, cords, picks, a strap, and a case. She made sure it was tuned properly before she left the store. Rangi and Nim helped her up on stage and got everything plugged in, and they were in business.

With the guitar, Tania suddenly felt like a whole person again, like she'd only been part of herself for years. She had to sell her Stratocaster her parents had bought her for Christmas in happier times. Tania had kept it locked up at school but had to sell it to pay for her first semester of college. Despite the scholarships and loans, there was just so damn much to pay for, and only so many hours in the day for her to be able to work. It didn't help that there were only shit jobs in the small town where she was, only so much money she could make.

The Stratocaster had been a gift, one of many that she later sold off to get her education. Plunging from upper middle class to living surrounded by farms didn't bother her as much as it probably should have, because she still had her Stratocaster. And, of course, Miss Amelia at the library. Now, she had a cheap knockoff, but at least she was herself again.

They got in, plugged in the equipment. Then, Flix surprised Tania by wanting to do "Dead or Alive." She was able to bang out the complex beginning to the song, shocking herself with the music coming alive under her fingers. Even with only singing the cowboy lyrics of a single song, Flix still had to leave the end of the song to her. Tania sang with wild abandon, able to hit notes she hadn't sung in years.

Tania was glad she had bought a little tripod for her phone while she was wandering around before the set. She had her cell phone record everything for the benefit of her sisters back home. Tania debated about recording "Rocket Queen," terrified that evil-minded Kandace would post it online, but she decided to trust, but threaten.

Tania didn't have to buy the champagne for "Pour Some Sugar on Me." One of the bartenders brought it over to her, and she gave him a saucy wink and a smile. He grinned back, and he sold several bottles right there on the floor. The audience roared the lyrics back at her, drank champagne by pouring it into each other's mouths, and asked for more and more curtain calls. They ended with "Close My Eyes Forever," went backstage to drink a lot of water, then went back out for another set.

Everyone completely vanished after the last set. Rangi was the only one to say, "See you next week." Tania grabbed her stuff, hauled it all two doors down for some tandoori chicken wraps and half a liter of chilled iced tea, washed up, hauled her equipment onto a *tuk tuk*, and managed to get everything inside her apartment, despite having to go through two key card doors.

Tania gargled with warm water to maintain her voice, then took a blessedly hot shower and washed out all of the hair goo. Post-shower, she found the hair goo online on her cell phone while drying her hair, ordered pots of the blue and silver wax, and the purple for good measure, and had it delivered. She put on underwear and a nightshirt and fell into bed.

～

*I*n the morning, Tania made the terrible mistake of emailing the concert footage, completely unedited, to her friends. She was barely through her mango and rice, washed down with another half-gallon of sweet tea, when Kandace and Corinne called.

"That Axel guy is dreamy," said Corrine.

"Not interested," said Tania. "Plus, he wears a wedding ring."

"Eww," said Corinne. "Hands off, I agree."

"Send pics of your hot boss," ordered Kandace. "We can't get this whole hair effect thing you're describing by looking at the website. Nice job, by the way. I even want to buy the stuff you have online, and I've got no damn room or need for it."

"Love the Lita Ford," opined Corinne.

"That's the raunchiest version of 'Rocket Queen' I've ever seen in my damn life," said Kandace. "And before you threaten me, no, I won't release this particular video into the wild. But, if I did, you'd have to quit your job and become a musician full-time."

"I happen to like my job," said Tania. "Plus, not a huge market for Thai hair bands. No, this is enormous amounts of fun, but I do have to remember to do this strange thing called sleeping. In fact, after I get off with you crazy bitches, I'm heading for the pool, then taking a nap."

"Show us the fake Stratocaster," said Corrine. Tania turned the volume all the way down on the amp, so the sound was only in the apartment. She played a little bit of "Sweet Child of Mine," and Corrine and Kandace clapped and cheered. Tania bowed; her friends' bitchy comments about her impromptu performance for them made her laugh so hard her cheeks and stomach hurt.

Tania said goodbye, put on her tankini, and went out to the pool. She floated awhile, got out and dried off, slathered on the sunblock, and set her phone alarm so she wouldn't broil herself if she fell asleep. She woke up to the alarm, managed to use the key cards correctly to get back to her apartment, took a quick shower, ate a mango and drank some more iced tea, and slept all the way through until the next morning.

~

Tania woke up ravenous at six in the morning, got ready for work, and did something she normally didn't do. She headed to McDonald's for breakfast. Then, she took her laptop to a co-working space and worked on her private marketing clients' online marketing needs. She arrived at work, cold strawberry iced tea in hand, and smiled and said hello to everyone. She sat down at her desk and whipped through more work in an hour than she normally did in three, resolutely keeping her hands on the keyboard. Touching her lips in memory of the scorching kiss would be a dead giveaway.

"Did you, what do the Americans say, hang out with your friends in Nimman?" Achara asked Lupe.

Lupe laughed. "I did. I had a little party at a hotel, introduced...I'll call him Drone. He's an office drone, needs to meet pretty women. I introduced him to...I'll call her Real Estate. He's not bad looking, so it worked." Achara thought this was romantic. Tania thought it was gossipy and a bit demeaning, but Lupe was so proud of herself and her skill at making introductions. The others talked about school and about buying new scooters with their hard-earned money.

Tania didn't talk about much of anything. Sanur came in, gave Tania a smile, then went directly to his office. He wasn't cold or rude, just a little evasive. Tania decided that her friends were right, and that he was covering his tracks after a terrible onstage heat-of-the-moment misstep and didn't want an angry holler girl screaming about sexual harassment. But that kiss had been *amazing*. She came back from a short juice break to find her new helmet under her desk, old clothes inside. That made her laugh.

Tania zipped through more work, took a long lunch, and then she and Lupe were both hit with numerous Spanish-speaking customers in love with the new African line. Tania only managed to keep hydrated and fed because Aat brought her the tea and food she needed.

The only hint Tania had that anyone else at work knew about her onstage antics over the weekend was when Aat whispered in her ear as she was leaving, "I didn't know you could play guitar." Tania tried not to cringe. No one else said anything to her about it. Tania said goodnight, ate street chicken and noodles on the way home, took a shower, and fell into bed. She fell asleep, her fake Stratocaster right by her bed where she could reach out and touch it in her sleep.

~

ania brought the guitar to the orphanage and taught them how math and music intersected. She taught them song lyrics, but nothing quite so risqué as "Rocket Queen," mostly Beatles tunes, the ones everyone knows and could sing in their sleep.

Then, Tania decided to head down to a practice place close to her apartment, paid for a small room, and played through as many '80s tunes as she could remember. She laughed as she stumbled over lyrics and chords, but slowly got her fingers and voice under control. Bit by bit, she found the old mojo coming back. She caught a *tuk tuk* home, and crashed in bed, still fingering chords as she fell asleep.

~

ork returned to normal, sometimes manic, sometimes a bit calmer. Sanur kept up his cone of silence and went off on two business trips in quick succession, one in Southeast Asia, one to Brazil with Lupe. Tania decided not to think about what was going on with her boss and pretended that they had the easy chemistry they had before. But there was something a little jagged about them now, a little bit of knowledge the two of them had about each other that they didn't have before. They didn't go out to lunch or dinner anymore, didn't crack little satiric jokes to each other. Tania tried not to drive herself crazy thinking about it and focused on work to pay off her loans and her new sheet music fix.

Tania bought more hard rock outfits with fake leather trim because real leather would suffocate her in the heat and took on a new online marketing client to pay for it. She practiced quietly at home and in full rock-goddess mode nearly every weekend.

Tania bought the bike she had been craving, a used delivery bike in black and red with a box on the back for her amp and cords. She could sling her guitar on her back and learned to zip through traffic despite her heart pounding through her chest and sweating through her gloves. She found a vented summer weight jacket to go with the brain bucket, a full-face helmet in a slick red and gold. She wore jeans and motorcycle boots and gloves with knuckle protectors, smothering herself in the heat. Tania had a job, volunteer work, the apartment, the pool, the workout room, and the band she wanted. She wasn't stupid enough to die in Thai traffic when she finally had it all.

PAYOFF

$\mathcal{D}$ue to a massive amount of work, and travel on Sanur's part, it was three weeks before Sanur and Tania had another dinner. The rain came down like a waterfall outside. They ate at an Indian restaurant and shared *samosas*, fried pastries with potato. Since they were catching up, they violated the no-work-talk-at-dinner rule with impunity.

Sanur ate another samosa, then narrowed his eyes at Tania. "I've been to three continents in three weeks, I haven't slept in my own bed in nearly a month. I haven't had delicious cooking like this in a while. I usually grab some street food and run to my next appointment. I feel like I've met every artistic collective in every country in the world."

Tania grinned. "There are over two hundred countries in the world, depending on who you ask. I doubt you have visited them all."

"I had to hire bodyguards several times, because local people thought I was doing... what, I'm not sure." Sanur sighed, drained his tea, poured more. "Selling arms? Drugs? I have no idea. I had drug-sniffing dogs sniff the samples I picked up more times than I can count. I took the products I purchased to local shippers and sent them to you, partly not to carry so much around, mostly because I was really tired of wasting so much time having people go through my suitcase and briefcase at airports and border crossings."

"Lupe and the interns thought it was Christmas with the attitude they had towards the boxes. I had to make Lupe stop taking photo shoots long enough to accept Spanish-speaking calls." Tania ate the last samosa and was delighted when the butter chicken and garlic naan bread showed up. She was ravenous, having worked through lunch.

Sanur laughed and bowed. "I am so delighted I could be of service. I filled up warehouses from Tanzania to Guyana, got all the tracking software installed, worked on decreasing lost and damaged items, and in general hired many people on this last trip. I met mayors and head people, I received the keys to some villages, and I have personally contacted and visited dozens of orphanages. I personally set up accounts with the greengrocers to have food delivered automatically every day. Several of the children have been hired as runners to carry the food back to the orphanages."

"I got the list." Tania paused from tearing off naan bread to pick up her chicken. "Food is a major thing, so your contacts were quite helpful. I made sure that we got cell phone videos of the kids actually eating the food paid for from their sales. I do not want the food to go in the wrong people's mouths."

Sanur raised his eyebrows at her attention to detail then took some garlic naan. "Thank you." She inclined her head. "We have already begun clearing the rubble from the property we purchased in Indonesia." One of Sanur's other businesses was a housing nonprofit that bought buildings devastated by earthquakes, floods, and other disasters and rebuilt them as low-cost housing with space for local businesses such as gyms, laundromats, and convenience stores on the ground floors in the Thai style. That business was run entirely separately from the artistic one; Sanur used his trips for both businesses.

Sanur put his tea down. "Remember how I said we needed to stay small? You spoke at a school, and now we have eager interns, students, and single parents."

Tania nodded. After the school speech, many students wanted to work for them. Tania set up an internship program that paid a minimal amount plus food and transportation and allowed students to come in and see how the office was run. Students from the poorest schools competed for the internships. She would have hired more orphans, but their English was so good from her training that they were working at hotels.

Sanur sipped more tea. "You proved me wrong. We can expand but not get too large."

Tania grinned. "I took Kannika on the Career Day speech. She told the story about finding the artist, the one that sells mirrors with gorgeous frames. She found out he was her father's friend from the village where they grew up. Now he's hired people to help him from the village, and Kannika has an honorary uncle! Not a dry eye in the house with that story."

Sanur smiled. "Yes, I was delighted to hear of her honorary uncle." He took another sip of tea. "I'm still willing to wear both hats when traveling, but I'm seriously considering handing over the artistic business to you and Lupe. What's your percentage of paying off your loan?"

Tania narrowed her eyes at him. She knew perfectly well he knew everything down to the Thai baht. "The African market that I brought in and run is doing fantastically well. Also, now we have plenty of interns to help so I'm spending less time doing photo shoots and more time doing actual marketing and sales. So, you know that I'm damn near paid off." Tania took a sip of her mint tea then sucked in a breath. "You were planning on handing over this business all along."

Sanur ate a bite of his delicious butter chicken. "Finally figured it out?"

"You do realize it gives me all of your headaches. I'm going to have to hire you to travel the world for me or have Lupe do it. The teens are still in school. But we have enough artists, I think. I can only be gone for long weekends, certainly not a week at a time."

Sanur took some more chicken and sipped his tea. He noticed and approved of how Tania always thought of how to improve their teenagers' lives. "I can't believe how lucky I was to find you. You have no idea how hard it really is to find such talent. Then you found Lupe, with a perceptive eye for people that is incredibly rare. You listened, you learned, you grew."

Tania looked Sanur in the eye. She took out her cell phone and put in a number. She divided it by another number and showed him the result. "This is how much our—soon to be my—business is worth. I'm up to eight percent of the gross, but I'll have to sell a kidney to buy half. Lupe isn't in the position to buy anything, because she is still paying off school loans, and she goes out drinking with her friends three or four times a week. Since I don't want to sell a kidney,, does this mean we will do the same thing, where you sell me half the company and I pay you back over time?"

Sanur chewed, watching the whirring behind Tania's eyes. She sat up straight, put in more numbers. "Remember, I still have to make enough of a living to take time off and travel. I'm also going to have to hire some new people. Or get some more interns."

Sanur steepled his fingers. "In case you have not noticed, you do the work of three people. You are worth three times the salary I paid you, so subtract all that off the total."

"You paid for my housing, medical and dental too."

"Part of the package. The schools you worked for in Korea paid your housing and health and dental insurance, did they not?"

"They did." Tania sighed. "But you can't say that is standard business practice here."

"It is when you are hiring someone from overseas. Companies also pay for children to go to school, and you could have been married with three kids. I would have had to pay for all of that, spousal housing, schools for children. You saved me a fortune."

Tania snorted. "Yeah, well, I'm taking over someone else's business, making sure it keeps hundreds of people fed and gives them somewhere to sleep at night, no pressure there, so having kids is going to have to wait a bit. Not that I don't want to adopt half the orphanage, but I do have a business to run."

Sanur felt his heart sing just a bit. *She does want children,* he thought to himself. He switched his face back to the hard-nosed businessman

Tania was expecting to see. "Pay yourself for all of the training you've done. Trainers get extra pay, and you get later-shift pay differentials where you are from, do they not?"

"You do have a point about the training. I've trained every single person there. Plus visiting the school then hiring the interns." Tania looked some things up on her cell phone and said, "I'm taking off the salary of a full-time trainer. That's pretty much what I've been doing since I got here. So I'm an internet marketing guru, I do the books so the accountant has something other than nonsense to look at, and I'm also the hiring manager and the trainer."

"You're also the public relations person, and you've completely reworked the website. You're also a new business manager, and have got us working in completely different continents, not just completely different countries." Sanur smiled slowly at Tania. "Now, pay yourself all those salaries for the eleven months you've been here. How much do you actually owe me?" Sanur finished off his half of the butter chicken, knowing that Tania would scrupulously calculate a number that would be fair and reasonable.

Tania poked buttons on her phone, looked up, and said, "You owe me more than what's left on my school loans," she said, stunned. "That's even paying myself by the hour for the website work."

"And how long did it take for you to pay me back for that?" asked Sanur. He smiled at her expression that combined shock and horror. "And, half the business, half the profits. Business has never been better, we're opening up new markets faster than we can service them, and my accountant wants to hire another accountant to help the tax attorney."

"Whoa." Tania stared at her boss, stunned. But he wouldn't be her boss for long.

Sanur did not like the fear in her eyes. "I do not think you understand how many people have better lives because of us. You kept the business afloat, then expanded it. You have the ability to hire the right people, to keep moving in the right direction."

"How will this work?" Tania asked, dazed.

"I shall keep a percentage, look things over, get paid for my travels bringing in new products for you. I will protect you from scams, because those people will begin to harass you now that a non-Thai name will be on the business paperwork. I will have to move offices, leave the current one as your showcase. I will steal one of the interns to run things and get a much quieter office where I can hear myself think. I know of a property just around the corner, the same builder, and I can get a discount on the rent. Same courtyard, more living space above for interns if they want it. I can show it to you after dinner."

"You either bought it or built it."

"I improved it, a duplicate of our current office." Sanur grinned over the rim of his teacup. "I like the fish in the pond. Also, I need my own office space to run my businesses. I've spent too much time on this one, and I have more that needs my attention."

Tania felt her heart drop. He was leaving? She couldn't see him every day? She put her fingers to her mouth, felt his phantom kiss there.

"Perhaps we can have lunch or dinner from time to time. You will still keep me on as a consultant, no?" Sanur asked, with a wicked grin on his face.

Tania crunched some more numbers and showed him her calculator. He added five percent, and they shook hands on the final amount. "I will have our attorney, because I assume you would like to keep the same one for your business, draw up the paperwork. We'll both look it over and sign at the beginning of next week."

"Nice doing business with you," said Tania. She stood and shook his hand. "I'll be right back," she said, and headed towards the restroom. Sanur amused himself by altering the number on the contract his attorney had already sent him and sent it back for review. He hadn't been off by much. The guilt he felt over realizing just how much work she had put in compared to how little he had paid her in exchange left him as he finally gave Tania her proper compensation.

The server had taken away the empty plates and refreshed the tea by the time Tania came back. "How are Kandace and Corinne doing?" Sanur asked, sipping from his tea.

"Very well," said Tania. "I'm afraid I frightened the staff here with my happy dance in the bathroom."

Sanur choked out a laugh, trying not to spew his tea. Once his face was under control and she had poured her own tea, he looked into her beautiful hazel eyes. "I was paying you about eight times less than I should have been paying you," he said quietly. "I should have known and done something about it. I let myself get overwhelmed with too many other projects, but, in my defense, you should have, as you Westerners say, kicked my ass."

Tania laughed. "You did me an enormous favor and saved me many years and many thousands of dollars in very useless interest payments. If it makes you feel any better, I was planning on approaching you with at least cutting the rest of my debt in half." Sanur nodded approvingly. "I also wanted to talk to you about the time we kissed. It could be seen as a sexual harassment thing."

Sanur very carefully put down his teacup. "I can only apologize," he said quietly. "You were up on stage, and you were absolutely stunning. I'd never seen anyone like that before, didn't know how that would turn you from a swan into a very beautiful dirty angel."

Tania blushed at the dirty-angel description and snorted. "Smooth, but accurate. Besides, I sort of kissed you first. Just a peck, not a toe-curling one, but I sexually harassed you first."

Wait, she had curling toes? What does that mean? Sanur asked himself. "I was overcome. I rarely lose control. And despite my previous behavior, the woman who worked here before who stole my money begged me for months before I gave in. I'm not the kind of man who sexually harasses his employees. If it makes you feel any better, I always considered you to be an equal. It didn't take long, after a mental shove in the correct direction, until I realized that you could be the one to take over this company. I've been grooming you for that ever since."

Tania shook her head slowly. "I didn't feel sexually harassed, but I went along with you avoiding me, avoiding talking about what happened that night. What we had was too electric, too passionate, something that could easily distract us, and I had bills to pay, and there are literally people counting on me—on us—to put food in their bellies. I know neither one of us could afford the distraction at the time."

Tania smiled sadly, and Sanur sighed. *That kiss was an amazing mistake*, Sanur thought. But Tania did seem to feel as he did. How, then, should they proceed?

Tania ducked her head, kicked her feet under the table like a little girl. "Then you started having dinners with myself and Lupe, I assumed to train us, but also because you wanted a buffer between the two of us."

"And half the young people you surround yourself with," said Sanur. "Lupe is truly lovely, beautiful, and special. But it didn't escape my notice that she prefers the company of women."

"She's bisexual, I think," said Tania. "I've only gone out with her and her friends twice. They drink like fish, and I have other things I'd rather do with my money and my time than watching other people get drunk." She held up a finger. "Just so you know, Lupe cuts herself off well before the end of the night, and she's never come to work drunk or stoned or anything else."

"That is now your problem, not mine," said Sanur. "For now, I will own half the business. It is your choice whether or not to whisper in Lupe's ear that she could own some more of the business if she paid off her school loans faster. I looked into combining her loans into one, but interest rates in Spain for college loans are nowhere near as horrific as they are in the United States. Even though it's not really your business, I can say that she's paying them off more quickly than it may appear from her lifestyle."

Tania nodded. "You're right. It's not my business."

Sanur made his voice tight so Tania would hear his warning. "Like you, she has other things that bring in money. Not all of the people she spends her time with are friends. They are sometimes clients she introduces to other clients. They do business with each other, and she gets a...shall we say, a finder's fee. She only works with people that she trusts and she knows will do an excellent job, and she's very good at what she does."

Tania's jaw hit the ground. "I see. I take it she introduces online friends to other online friends in the real world?" Sanur nodded, and Tania laughed. "She's a mover! A shaker! A fixer!"

"Nimman is very much its own little community, and there are diamonds in the rough, so to speak. There are digital nomads with actual businesses. She brings people like travel vloggers, hoteliers, and adventure seekers together, things like that." Sanur smiled at the look of wonder on Tania's face.

Tania's jaw dropped. "That little skank, keeping things from me! She built her own entrepreneurial digital nomad introduction business right under my nose." Sanur watched the wheels moving in Tania's head once more. "Come to think of it, this is the perfect place to do that. This is where they are after all, their hunting grounds. Might as well get them all together, let all the parties get to know each other."

"You make them sound like wolves and lions meeting each other on the savanna, making introductions at the watering hole," said Sanur. "And what is a 'skank'?"

Tania laughed. "It should be mountain lions and wolves meeting each other. Wolves are cold weather predators, and lions are hot weather, and from different continents. And a skank is...the kind of woman I dress like when I perform on stage."

Sanur laughed, and put down his cup again before he spilled tea all over himself. "I have seen your 'Pour Some Sugar on Me' performance. So, that is what a 'skank' is?"

"The lyrics of the song actually call me a 'tramp' and a 'video vamp', which is close enough." She laughed, and said, "I need something stronger." She called over a server and ordered a Coke. Not a rum and coke, just a Coke. To her, "stronger" meant caffeine and sugar.

Sanur found himself laughing again, in wonder that he found this woman so far from her home. Of course, he was far from his home as well, having spent most of his youth in Bali. He missed the sound of the waves, the smell of salt in the air. He had considered moving there to run his many businesses, but he would wait for her for as long as it took.

"I will not date you tonight. When you sign the papers and own half the business, then it will not be sexual harassment if we choose to date. Then, when I'm actually in town, and you're not performing or teaching children, then I would like to spend time with you." Sanur smiled as her jaw dropped, and that light he loved to see came up in Tania's eyes. "I like many kinds of food, I like to dance, or we can simply walk around the city, or even lay still and watch a movie. I will do what you want when you want it, as long as it's something I can stand. I'm not going to do bungee jumping, cliff diving, or any other risky procedure. I prefer not to put myself at risk, because other people are counting on me."

"Oh, honey." Tania looked into his eyes. Sanur froze, afraid she was about to destroy his carefully-laid plans for her. Tania had never called him "honey" before. It seemed to be a term of endearment in the movies he had watched to try to understand Tania and where she had come from. "Kandace had friends like that for a hot minute; they scared me half to death. Well, I did the cliff diving, but that was an aberration. No, I plan on doing all my activities on the ground, unless we go to some tower that looks down on things, like the Petronas Tower in Kuala Lumpur. That would be kind of nice. And yes, I will date you. Once the company is half mine, of course." She grinned, eyes shining.

Sanur smiled back and bowed a little. "I accept your conditions."

"I'm not finished," said Tania. Sanur smiled at her hard-nosed attitude. He and his kind used tongues, not noses, but it was the same thing. She had a scent for business. "I won't make the same mistakes I made before, being paid less than I'm worth, half killing myself to prove myself. I have already proven myself, and you're selling me half your business because I have proven that to you. As you said, I am your equal. I'm probably younger than you, from what you told me I'd say about six years younger than you. But I'm most definitely anyone's equal."

Sanur stared at her. "I accept all your conditions," he said, his tone serious. "I do hope we can take buying trips together, but just letting you know, that's not a thin veil for an actual vacation. I do a lot of real work on those trips, but I do like to take a day or two and look around and enjoy what I'm seeing. I don't plan on spending my entire life on planes. There are some places I'd really like for you to see, and I hope at some point that you will go with me."

"That would be lovely. As for tonight, you can take me dancing for an hour and a half. After that, I'm going to go home and fall down on my bed, alone. And no kissing. If we do that, I'll forget that I have work tomorrow, and that's going to go very badly for both of us."

Sanur held up both hands in capitulation. "At this point, you make the rules. Later on, I'll probably have one or two of my own, but most of it's just common sense. I think we're both too old and wise to engage in the useless, petty, stupid games most people play in their relationships. I very literally do not have time for that."

"Now that I own half a company, neither do I."

Tania finished her tiny can of Coke, and Sanur gave his credit card to a passing server. "I'll be right back," Sanur said quietly. "We have a time crunch, and I know a place that you're going to love."

Sanur took his life into his hands when he rode on the back of her scooter. She had lightning-quick reflexes that saved their lives more than once. He directed her to a club, and she laughed when she realized they were playing '80s music. While she danced to Alannah Myles' song "Black Velvet," Sanur wondered how he could keep his hands off of her until the papers were signed. For now, he kept his hands on her swaying hips, her legs strong from Muay Thai kickboxing, and they danced until they were ready to drop.

～

The next afternoon, Kannika smiled at Tania. "Thank you for speaking at our school on Career Day. Everyone was sick of shops, tourism, restaurants, hotels, construction, tour guides, divers, people to watch after the children. We do so much more here."

Tania smiled. "They loved the story of the honorary uncle."

"What story?" Lupe asked.

"I found the woodcarver, the one who carves those gorgeous mirror frames. And I get a percentage of each sale, which makes the woodcarver happy, because we are distantly related. I call him Uncle now, and he is showing me how to carve. He was my father's friend. He says that he is very sorry about the motorcycle accident that killed my parents and is very horrify that no one stepped forward. Now I have an honorary uncle, and it is because of you."

"Horrified," Tania corrected Kannika without really thinking about it. "Great choice of words. Someone's been studying her word of the day. So what have you learned here?"

Kannika pulled up an ad, tapped it on the screen. "This ad brings in almost four hundred American dollars in profits a week. I designed it, and now I get a percentage of those profits."

"So, sales, marketing, profit-sharing, and spotting local artists. When you went on photo shoots, did you learn anything?"

Kannika lowered her voice. "I learned color, composition, formatting, backgrounds, which camera to use and why, lighting, and so much more every time I go. We hate the lottery system. Every time we learn something, we don't go back for another two weeks as the other people rotate through. Why don't you have us on for a week then off for a week? Everyone has been... What do you say? Cross-trained."

Tania held up a finger and thought a minute. "Sure, go to a week-on rotating schedule." Kannika cheered soundlessly, waving her arms, which made Tania grin. "If there's any takeaway I wanted you to get from this, it's cross-training. The more you learn, the more valuable you are to me, and Sanur and Lupe, and to this company. And the more you bring to your classes, because you have more knowledge. And the sadder we're going to be when you do the whole college thing and leave us behind."

Kannika grimaced. "You want me to spend thousands of dollars of my own money to get a degree in business. Why? Didn't you go to college, and then teach me, teach all of us, what you learned by running this business? Wouldn't that apply to any business? So why do we have to go to school if we already learned it here?"

Lupe nodded her head. "The young woman has a point." Lupe raised her hand when Tania pretended to lunge across the desk at her. "Wouldn't you agree that this young woman has learned more than either one of us learned in school? I'm not disparaging my art degree. The problem is, I didn't see real-world applications until I met you. I wanted to work in a gallery, an auction house, a museum. I had no idea that the competition was so fierce for those jobs, the number of degrees and certifications that would be required."

Tania calmed down. She could see Lupe's point. "I see that. Knowledge versus real-world application."

Lupe pointed to her own computer. "Here, I get to work with the artists themselves, use the Internet and my language skills, and my skills in composition, lighting, and photography to bring those artists to the world. I can't think of something more rewarding."

"I think that's a point," said Tania. "How much of what we learned had real-world applications? That's not to say I didn't really enjoy learning the guitar and drums." The others laughed. Although it embarrassed the hell out of her, everyone had been by to see Tania's rock goddess performances. She didn't perform every weekend, didn't even get together with the band every week, but she practiced like a real rocker and was getting really good, or at least much better.

"Knowledge is a really good argument for attending school. But did I really need to learn the works of every master in history to do my current job? Even following your plan, and yes, I know, I go out too much, it will still take me another two years to pay off my debts." Lupe made a face. "Certificates are the key. You should be able to build up enough to get in at least an associate's degree, if not a bachelor's degree."

Tania nodded. "Most businesses that make money these days are online or have an online component. If you don't know how to run your own website, put up ads, or write blogs, you're in big trouble in the real world now. And so many people with degrees have their own businesses, and they have to hustle to learn this on their own because a lot of colleges just don't teach this stuff." She grinned as phones rang; they picked them up and began to help their customers.

ISLAND DAYS

Sanur called his travel agent and got a booking to Boracay in the Philippines for Tania. He upgraded her to business class and told Tania to go away and not come back for a week. Tania had been looking pale and had made silly mistakes. She corrected them quickly, but it was obvious she was exhausted. He told her to book whatever hotel rooms she liked, to do whatever she wanted to do. He gave her a prepaid credit card loaded with a thousand dollars and told her to be sure that card was empty when she returned.

Sanur closed the office for a week and sent the orphans to Pattaya for fun in the sun with a trusted friend, the majordomo who ran his own home, Htet. Before they flew out, he, Tania, and the quad helped move the orphanage to a much bigger location. He also paid for protein five times a week, taking this job away from Tania, and made sure the orphans ate at least three meals a day, either at school or at home. The orphans were delighted, especially when they got rooms with actual bunk beds, and Sanur felt the fear and confusion from his past floating away as he helped the orphans flourish.

Sanur walked Tania to a *tuk tuk* for the airport. "Please relax, and don't have a single thought of work."

"I'll take a lot of pictures and text them to my friends and to you if you'd like them." Tania was dressed for fun, with khaki shorts, a teal top, and sunglasses. Her red-gold hair was pulled back in a braid and glinted in the sun.

"I would." Sanur put her backpack on the seat, handed her up, and gave her a quick kiss on the cheek. "Enjoy yourself, relax. The quad is on break too, and I'm headed to Bali to visit friends. Go away, don't look back." She nodded and waved as the *tuk tuk* driver drove away.

~

*T*he flight was delayed, but Tania didn't mind. It was Tania's first real vacation where she wasn't trapped in a country, taking only a few days off, desperately trying to pay off her school loans. With her cut of the profits, Tania was delighted that she had already paid off a quarter of her loan from Sanur. She read, played video games while waiting for the flight, and relaxed so much she fell asleep on the plane.

She landed in the Philippines in the driving rain in Manila, transferred to a smaller plane to Caticlan, took a boat, and went to her hotel. It turned out the hotel had been overbooked, so she simply walked down the street until she found another hotel with a beautiful courtyard. She was stunned to find out she could get a huge room with a ceiling fan for less than the other hotel. She put her backpack on the huge bed covered by a mosquito net, turned on the ceiling fan to circulate the air, and came back down, ravenous.

In the courtyard over drinks and bowls of grilled chicken and rice, she met a woman named Lupe from Spain living in the Philippines because of the lower cost of living there. Lupe had a fall of chestnut hair held at the bottom with a golden clip, a wide smile, a deep laugh, and a gentle demeanor. Tania felt that she had instantly made a friend.

They made a plan to go surfing at another beach from the one in front of them. The hotel's host called his *tuk tuk* driver cousin and promised the cousin would be ready for them early in the morning, along with sliced fruit for breakfast and some juice. They exchanged stories of living abroad for about two hours, then Tania, tired from the trip, went in to get some sleep.

In the morning after breakfast, the *tuk tuk* came to take them where they wanted to go. They watched the sunrise, and they stood by the water in front of a white stone temple with numerous pillars, watching the sun rise just above the temple's tower piercing the sky.

Their surfing instructor was a muscular guy named Ramon. They hit the waves, and Tania fell off a million times. By the end of their two-hour lesson, Tania was exhausted. She paid the man and stumbled off to get a watermelon shake, chicken on a stick, and some rice.

They decided to wander back towards their hotel. Lupe regaled Tania with the story about a drunken best friend and a stolen violin. Lupe stopped, pretended to be Lara Croft from Tomb Raider, and did a flip off a tree onto the ground. "So you're a violinist and a gymnast?" asked Tania.

Lupe laughed. "I played the violin in middle and high school. I've been a receptionist about eight times since I've graduated from college. I need to rise up; I can't be receptionist forever. I have a degree in art history, which doesn't seem to be conducive to having a job."

"Have you ever thought about living in Thailand?"

"What? Why?"

"I do marketing for a small company. Actually, I run the office in Chiang Mai, Thailand. The company sells art and furnishings from the poor people who make them, enabling them to feed their families. I think you'd be excellent at setting up the photo shoots and doing customer service for Spanish-speaking customers. We have clients in sixteen Spanish-speaking countries. Do you speak Portuguese?"

"Yes, I do." Lupe's dark brown eyes opened wide. "My grandfather is Portuguese. I grew up speaking both languages. In fact, I've spent more time in Lisbon then I have in Madrid."

"Our clients use our products in their homes, or when selling a home to decorate it to make it beautiful." Tania pulled up and showed

Lupe the website on her phone, and Lupe pulled it up on her own phone.

Tania took dozens of pictures of the beach and made a short video for her friends Kandace and Corinne, while Lupe wandered around the online site. Her sister-friends had liked Tania's pictures about living in South Korea, but they seemed entranced with her life in Thailand. She sent the pictures out to her friends and sent some to Sanur and the quad as well.

Tania bought them some frozen lime juice from a shop. Lupe caught up, her anklets creating a slight ringing sound as she walked. Tania handed her a cup of frozen goodness. "I'm in," Lupe said. "You have some very beautiful things on your website. Selling them won't be a problem."

Tania laughed. "You haven't even heard about a salary yet!"

"So what's the salary?" asked Lupe.

"You can either get a free apartment and one percent of the gross, or you can get a flat salary."

"How much is one percent?" asked Lupe. Tania did some fast calculations on her cell phone and held out the amount on the calculator app. Lupe grinned. "Shit!" she yelled. "You had me at free apartment, you idiot!"

"Did I tell you that the apartment has a pool?"

"You are a crazy person," said Lupe. "You don't even know me. I think you are one of those *loca* women."

"You could be as well." Tania shrugged. "The worst we would be out is a few hundred dollars for the free apartment. We only pay three months in advance."

"Okay! I'll do it!" Lupe began salsa dancing on the beach.

Tania laughed. "No more talking about it until we're on the plane home. And then you'll have a few days to acclimate yourself in Thailand before you start your new job."

"Anything you say." Lupe did a spin of happiness, making Tania laugh.

They wandered around, going in and out of shops, buying little artistic things, until it was time to get dinner. They found their *tuk tuk* driver again, but Tania asked him to wait because she found a young boy selling beautiful art. She got the boy's name and an email address and bought a small painting that she rolled up and put into her small daypack.

Lupe thought this was a game and found another woman selling beautiful carvings. Lupe got an actual phone number and an email address, and Tania bought several of the woman's tiny beautiful carvings of elephants, banyan trees, and temples.

They fed their *tuk tuk* driver and themselves while they were wandering around finding new artists, then he brought them back to the hotel. The ladies walked around until they found another restaurant they liked. They dined on some amazing veggie skewers and noodles and spent half the night chatting as if they were little girls at camp.

They took a day trip to the stunning Ariel's Point for snorkeling, kayaking, and cliff diving. They walked around the island, sampling the sights and sounds. The sidewalks were filled with vendors and parked motorcycles.

They wandered all over and eventually found the night market. They found several people who were selling things that Tania definitely wanted to sell online. They both got a lot of pictures of the things that were available. There were some excellent items that would be perfect for the website. They found an old man selling stone carvings, bought a few, and got his grandson's email address. They got several business cards and went back to their hotel laden with net bags stuffed with very small purchases.

That night, they slept for nearly eleven hours straight, exhausted from all the walking and swimming. The next day, after a quick fruit breakfast, they swam and laid around at the beach. When it got hot, they went to a museum and had a wonderful time exploring all of the objects there. Exhausted, they went back to the night market for food and drinks and to sit on a mat to relax in the evening breeze.

They swam, rested under umbrellas on lounge chairs, ate delicious four-dollar meals including a drink, danced the night away in little clubs, and greatly enjoyed wandering the beach and all around. They woke up, ate, swam, dried off, ate more, drank a lot of coconut milk, and laughed at every opportunity. They relaxed and enjoyed every minute and were sad to board the plane to Thailand.

~

Sanur greeted them at the airport. "I am delighted to meet you," he said to Lupe.

"I told him all about you," Tania said with a smile.

"I have already done a background check. Let's head to the office and get a contract signed. Come. I have a taxi waiting." Tania followed Lupe and Sanur, who were happily chatting. They went to the office, and Lupe read her contract and signed it while Tania fished out the larger artwork from their luggage to show Sanur later, along with all the contact information. She left two of the smaller things in her suitcase.

"Lupe, I'm going to take you to the visa office now. We need to add the contract to the working visa." He turned to Tania. "You must be tired."

Tania shrugged. "Let's leave the bags here, and I can train Lupe using my cell phone on some things while we're waiting to get this done." The wait wasn't too long, then a *tuk tuk* brought them back to the office to pick up the baggage.

Lupe's apartment was in another building but also nearby the office. Lupe's pool was slightly smaller, but her apartment had a bigger gym on the first floor. "This is amazing!" Lupe said. She hugged Tania. "Thank you!"

Tania laughed. "Thank the boss man, here."

"*Muchas gracias.* Thank you very much!"

Sanur stepped back, concerned about receiving an attack hug. "You are very welcome."

They left Lupe to acclimate, then Sanur walked Tania back to her apartment. On the way back, Tania showed Sanur the smaller objects she had brought back. "Lovely. You have a good eye."

"Actually, Lupe notices even more than I do. She has an amazing eye." He took note of all of the artists, and once she was at the main door, he walked away from Tania's apartment building and immediately started sending texts.

Tania made it into the elevator and down the hall to her apartment with her laden backpack, dropped the pack just inside the door, took a shower, and went to bed. She took the next day off, hung out by the pool, and ate street food for lunch and dinner. She was exhausted, so she went to bed early.

~

Tania woke up the next day refreshed and rejuvenated. She went into work, hugged everyone, and set out to find out how things had gone in her absence. Everyone enjoyed their vacations, and they talked about beaches in between phone calls.

Tania had told Lupe to sleep in; all the traveling was exhausting. Tania worked on a new ad campaign, then Lupe came in for lunch and met everyone. Lupe had studied the product line nonstop while on the plane. Tania trained her on the telephone script and was pleased when Lupe asked intelligent questions. Lupe was delighted to take her first Spanish-speaking call. When she hung up the call she said, "I sold...in dollars, four hundred fifty!" She stood up and danced a little salsa. Achara put her hand over her mouth and laughed.

Tania grinned. "Don't get cocky, kid."

Lupe narrowed her eyes. "I will upsell you."

"Outsell," Tania said. "Outsell means you sell more. Upsell means you get people to buy more little things, which is how you outsell me."

"I will do both," Lupe promised.

"You're on," Tania said. They bumped fists.

Sanur took everyone out to dinner, and they laughed at each other's stories of their travels. It was as if Lupe had always been there, from the very first day.

⁓

*T*ania found the new schedule to be very interesting. She swam in the mornings after her workouts right after her morning meditation when she would be too tired to argue with herself about whether or not to work out. She ate fruit and noodles for breakfast at a time that was previously her lunch. She worked on her own marketing clients, then went into work.

Lupe took a lot of work off her shoulders. Lupe came in a little later than their opening time to hit up more of the Spanish and Portuguese-speaking clients. She wore a noise-canceling headset with a very long range and would pace all over the office, even out into the courtyard, racking up enormous sales. Tania always knew when she made a huge sale because she would dance the salsa.

Lupe ordered some frighteningly expensive equipment and put up some rattan walls in a corner of the second floor near a window, turning it into a set for photoshoot extravaganzas. She was often there in the early morning when the light was just right, doing shoots with the teenage boys. She had them hopping like frogs but slipped them extra money and fed them well. Tania had the girls circulate in on the shoots to learn the skill from a professional.

They had many new artist-clients from Boracay, and they found lots of new products to showcase, such as paintings, weavings, carvings, jewelry, and lightweight furniture made from wood. Lupe took pictures of them, and Sanur loved it all.

Tania concentrated on the online marketing, making the photo shoots count in a variety of social media ads. She also did all of the sales tracking, and was pleased to realize that they were grossing far more money since Lupe came in.

⁓

*T*hree weeks after Lupe started, Sanur took Lupe on a tour of Central and South America to find new undiscovered artisans that made products that could be sold worldwide. Sanur specialized in orphanages around the world. He found a great deal of raw talent, and a way to benefit teenagers who needed to find a way in the world before they were kicked out on the street. Girls, especially, were denied an education and even became victims of sex trafficking. Tania and Lupe fully supported Sanur in preventing that horrible crime from happening by buying work from these young artisans.

While Sanur and Lupe were gone, a young woman named Aaliyah Netsebe from the Democratic People's Republic of the Congo sent Tania a YouTube style video with many local artists, many of them single women. Aaliyah included a phone number, and Tania gave her a call after checking the time zone first. "Hello, this is Tania Brussell from Kaung Import-Export for The Home. May I speak to Aaliyah Netsebe?"

"Tania! It is Aaliyah. Did you like the products?"

"I like them so much that I want one of each!" Tania said. "Please email me a product list with prices and your PayPal. I'll give you a shipping tracking number, and that will pay the shipper for both packing and shipping for anything you want to send."

"That is amazing," Aaliyah said. "I had hoped...this is beyond anything I had hoped. The women...they must feed their families. So many have nothing. I mean, really nothing. We have formed a collective to keep everyone alive." She sighed, and Tania heard the tears in her voice.

"Please take pictures, lots of pictures, of your fabrics. I would like to use them to make logos for the product line. Your textiles are amazing, and I can use the colors as backdrops for the ads. We'll add the cost of shipping to the prices, and you'll just use the tracking number I'll give you so that shipping is free for you." Tania saw that she had already received an email with the products and prices. She went over it as she listened to Aaliyah cry from joy.

A week later, Tania ended up with everything from paintings to tapestries, wood carvings to jewelry, even beautifully painted tiles, from DNR Congo. Sanur and Lupe, exhausted from their trip, loved what had been sent. Sanur told Tania to do as she wished, that the African line would be hers.

Tania put up a completely new page on the website, contacted free trade initiatives who in turn contacted artisans all over the enormous African continent, and soon Tania had to fill whole segments of the warehouses just on the African things from DNR Congo, Kenya, Nigeria, Senegal, Ethiopia, Somalia, Rwanda, Ghana, Niger, Zimbabwe, Uganda, and Tanzania with plans to acquire items from other countries as they went along.

Tania used Lupe's equipment and her own artistic eye to showcase the products from Africa and ran special ads. At first, the income from this line trickled in, but as more and more people gave stellar online reviews about the artistry of the products, the sales climbed up and up, quadrupling in a single month.

～

T he sun was beginning to set on another scorching day in Lagos. The noise in the restaurant on the first floor of Sanur's hotel was not quite deafening, from patrons, wait staff, faint shouts from the kitchen, the noise of the traffic outside. The air-conditioning worked and the hotel had a backup generator. The restaurant, one of the best, served *kilishi*, marinated, sun-dried meat, and *dambu namba*, shredded chicken served in vegetable "cups." The drinks were ice-cold, part of why Sanur had picked the restaurant and this hotel. Sanur ordered Coke. The local Nigerian alcohol drink, *ogogoro*, was fermented palm tree juice. Sanur did not want to end up under the table, so he avoided the drink. The Coke came quickly. He ordered another one with lime when he saw an unexpected visitor cross the room and sit directly in front of him.

Supayalat looked cool in a golden linen sheath dress. Sanur

wondered where she had hidden her knives and decided they were probably in her upswept black hair. Sanur wore khaki pants and a light blue linen shirt, setting off his coppery skin in the lingering light of dusk. "Why are you here?" Sanur asked his vassal and cousin. He had expected her to be searching for the missing Somchair and Malee. Betrayals could not be allowed to stand.

"You need a bodyguard. They think you are some warlord paying your way through drugs or black market goods, going into the poorest sections of town with impunity, spending money on motor-cycle couriers."

Sanur sipped his drink. He had no idea why a blend of artificial substances could taste so good after a day finding artists and their wares. "They do? Very well. The trail has gone cold?"

"I will find them." Supayalat narrowed her eyes. "And they will regret it very much when I do. I hope they circle back. I would like to catch them in Thailand."

Sanur nodded. "I can see why." The prisons there were no joke. The food arrived, and they spoke of long flights and street fairs.

Then Supayalat said something that made Sanur believe he had been drinking *ogogoro* without his knowledge. "You are fascinated by this woman, this Tania." Supayalat rolled the unfamiliar vowels around in her mouth.

"I...respect her. She acquires knowledge at an ever-increasing pace. She runs the business in my absences, which are too frequent as of late. She has my trust." He narrowed his eyes, frustrated that his vassal had caused him to speak of business during dinner. He became very still. He had danced with Tania, and had been entranced and seduced, in the style of his people. He had fallen into a deep well and was disturbed that he did not want to set himself free.

"Do you wish to bed her?" Supayalat ordered more Cokes.

Sanur nearly sprayed his vassal with his Coke. He swallowed, choked, swallowed again. "Tania...she is worth more than that. In her world, such a response would be a criminal act. I am her employer. In her world, this is not done unless between those of different depart-ments in a large company or between equals."

Supayalat took the new Cokes from the server and nodded. The young man withdrew. "Then make her your equal." Sanur sat back and ate the rest of the meal in silence, mind whirring. As always, Supayalat served him in the best ways. She made him think.

A man with a narrow body and eyes that swept everywhere sat at Sanur's table without permission. Supayalat had a knife against his leg under the table before he could say a word. "Be careful, hyena," she hissed.

The man held up his wide hands. "You are the ones in our territory without permission."

Sanur snorted. "Do you know who I am?" The man shook his head. "My name is Sanur. My family has been in existence for a thousand years more than your lines. I am not here to poach in your territory. Do not cross me, ever. We...squeeze our opponents dry. Do you understand?"

The man shook his head then laughed, a high-pitched, crazy sound. "We have numbers."

"And we, guile." Sanur narrowed his eyes to slits, let the vertical pupils come up from his false human eyelids. "Fool. I come to help the poorest among you have a better life. Now, go, if you and your kind wish to live."

Supayalat did something with her other hand, and the man fell off his chair onto the ground. "Go." She let her eyes change, just for a second. The man rose, brushed himself off, and melted into the crowd. Supayalat sighed. "We must go after dinner. They will be back, in numbers."

"Pity. I hoped to help more artists here." Their food came. They ate quickly and melted into the night.

～

Sanur shouldn't have been surprised about the meeting place. It was an elegant room overlooking the square. There were expensive couches, small golden tables for those who wished to stand, a low table in front of the couch, and a wet bar. Lights glowed in the darkness outside the windows. They could see half the city from where they were. King Karatu was wearing black pants, thousand-dollar shoes, and a golden shirt open at the neck to display a ruby necklace. He wore ruby rings on his fingers. He looked cool, composed, elegant. His mane of black hair streaked with gold moved as he surveyed the room and when he spoke.

A young woman dressed all in black, braids clacking, was there with drinks, a small smile on her face. The young woman smiled and inclined her head when Supayalat, leaning on the wall just inside the door, refused a drink.

Supayalat kept one eye on Sanur, the other one on Queen Khaledi. The queen leaned against the back of the couch, arms crossed. She wore gold and black, just like her husband. Golden bracelets ran up and down both arms, and her earrings were like small chandeliers.

Queen Kinva was shorter than both her husband and Khaledi, smaller, with a longer neck. All her jewelry was silver. She had a face even more elegant and refined than the king's first wife. Queen Kinva leaned against a bar stool, those fierce whiskey eyes missing nothing.

Sanur wasn't stupid enough to eye the young server. If King Karatu had caught him staring at what was obviously one of his daughters, Sanur may end up losing body parts. The king's other daughters were impressive. Two of them were in medical school, and the third was a famous chef. This one must be Lhia, the youngest. Lhia smiled, then went behind the bar in a sweep of hair and hips.

Like her husband, Queen Khaledi's hair was ebony with gold tips, braided like her daughter's on one side. Like Sanur, the color of her hair didn't come from a bottle. Queen Khaledi raised a golden finger-nail. "Let me check my understanding, Mr. Kaung. Or shall I say Your Highness?"

Sanur waved away the title with the pinkie finger of his right hand. Lhia came back to him, and he received the lime Coke in a rocks glass with grace. The glass was heavy, obviously crystal. He inclined his head and waited until Lhia finished doling out drinks and left with another swish of her hips. Sanur prudently kept his eyes on his glass.

Queen Khaledi inclined her head slightly, making her hair on the right sway as if in a nonexistent breeze. "You want these motorcycle roads of yours built through our territory."

Sanur inclined his head. "The roads benefit everyone. Motorcycles and electric bicycles go through the middle, and people can walk on the sides. They will be built in the Roman way, with the best drainage."

Khaledi raised her eyebrows. "That will be expensive."

Sanur nodded. "Of course. But these roads have to last through heat and torrential rains. The villagers will be better able to move themselves around and bring their products to market."

Khaledi nodded again. "You'll be cutting through clans and tribes that don't trust one another. You will have workers that don't speak each other's languages."

Sanur raised one shoulder. "I hire intermediaries. Speakers. Surely you have those."

"We do." Queen Khaledi looked thoughtful.

Queen Kinva nodded once. "And the medical clinics? The schools?"

Sanur inclined his head. "Every fifty kilometers." Sanur sipped from his drink as he enjoyed the shock on the younger queen's face.

Queen Khaledi regally shook her head. "Twenty-five."

"Schools or clinics?" asked Queen Kinva, the silver, black, and red beads in her waist-length braided hair clacking.

Sanur looked at Supayalat out of the corner of his eyes. She texted and flashed a five and a zero with her fingers. Sanur was stunned and delighted. One of his family's ancient palaces had been carefully and lovingly brought back to its former glory and would be used as a retreat and training center. The yoga and martial arts masters had ensured that the property would be filled year-round with acolytes and practitioners and carefully maintained. He had been negotiating for a twenty-five year lease but was stunned at the offer of fifty years.

Sanur waved the tips of his fingers. Supayalat's fingers flew, then she gave a tiny nod. "Both, alternating every twenty-five kilometers to start." Sanur gave a small smile and sipped his cola. The queens were sipping chai tea, the king Red Bull. Sanur would have preferred the tea, but he needed the sugar and caffeine because he was about to fly out that evening.

"Then twenty-five later?" asked Queen Kinva.

Supayalat flashed the ancient symbol for "d" with her fingers. Sanur realized she was talking about the apartment building in Da Nang. He flicked a fingernail back at her and angled his chin slightly. His vassal lowered her eyes to her screen again, thumbs flying across the keys.

The king began to pace, growling under his breath. "How are we going to staff all of this?"

Queen Khaledi nodded. "We will have to inform the villages that they must send their children out to be doctors and teachers." She took off one of her bracelets and handed it to her husband. "Use this for the first scholarship."

The king took the bauble from his wife's hand. "You humble me with your generosity."

Supayalat flashed an "a" with her fingers at Sanur. Sanur was delighted. In Da Nang, an Argentinian chef with a nearby restaurant and his front of house manager Vietnamese wife literally had more money coming in that they knew what to do with. They had been negotiating the last items in the sale. The apartment house would be filled with people who worked in the surrounding restaurants. It was a fantastic investment. "If we use buildings that are built off-site and moved, put together like jigsaw puzzles, we can have both. My people can teach your construction workers how to assemble them."

The king nodded. "If they will withstand the rains, then yes. This is a good idea." He waved his hand, literally pushing that problem aside. "Security is the real problem, building sites and all along the roads."

Sanur nodded. "Use the hyenas."

The king guffawed. "I thought you had a problem with them. Your retainer was quite insistent about them not putting their noses into your business."

Sanur shrugged. "If they can keep the warlords out and prevent children working when they should be in school, then why not use them?"

The king threw back his head and laughed, a rich, throaty sound that came from the belly. "I understand. Just know that the hyenas don't respect anyone."

Sanur inclined his head. "I understand they will not work for free. Security is built into the budget of every road." Supayalat flashed her fingers. The apartment building had been sold, so funding was no longer an issue.

Queen Khaledi hissed. "There will be no child labor. We have worked night and day to stamp out this scourge. I will personally see to it that the children are in school and not working on the road."

Queen Kinva nodded. "I will be where you are not."

Queen Khaledi touched Queen Kinva's hand. "I will use you as you have offered. This project will take many years."

Sanur shrugged. "Nothing worthwhile is fast or easy. Or inexpensive."

The king roared with laughter. "I like you, snake. I did not believe that would be true. Come, let us work out a contract with what we have decided here." Sanur inclined his head, and Supayalat sent the queens and king the contract.

~

When Sanur got back, he took Tania out to lunch. Sanur ordered pad thai, then complained. "I have had to pay for a fleet of motorcycle messengers driven by locals. They can carry the smaller materials and finished products in less time over bumpy roads than trucks."

"Aaliyah was very happy to meet you! She sent me an email. You put in a huge order! Aat and Chai got busy taking even more pictures." She grinned. The boys were getting very good at photography, and so were the girls.

"I met forty-two artist collectives. Each collective now has bicycles and motorcycles. I own a company that gets materials and hires local people to build wind, water, and solar systems to where people in rural areas need power to make their products. The collectives all have power now."

"Impressive," Tania said, a bit stunned. She knew Sanur had other businesses but hadn't attempted to find out what they were.

"The collectives help all of them to afford to send their children to school and for new supplies for more products." Sanur grinned. He looked deeply tanned, happy, and very satisfied, but extremely exhausted.

"We really are keeping people alive, aren't we?"

Sanur grinned. "Now you see why this company exists."

"I do," said Tania. She felt the tears pricking her eyelids.

Sanur smiled at her. "Do not cry. Beautiful women should not have tears, except for joy."

Tania blushed and grinned. "This is definitely joy." She stared at him as the words sunk in. "Wait. You think I am beautiful?"

Sanur smiled gently. "If you do not, then you are a fool. And, you have proven to me many times that you are not a fool."

Wait, my super-rich globetrotting boss thinks I'm beautiful! Tania *squeed* inside but tried to imitate Sanur's regal nature. "Thank you." She smiled at him over the rim of her glass.

Sanur's heart stuttered in his chest. He decided to be sure she always saw herself as beautiful. He had no idea how to accomplish that, but he decided to try.

Sanur thought of himself as a solitary man, equally comfortable on planes and on the ground, in one country or another. He didn't stay in five-star hotels, because why spend money there that could be better spent on his artists and orphans? He had a cell phone, so he could do business anywhere.

That's why his businesses prospered where others failed. Others wanted to spend money on fancy cars, private planes, expensive hotels, bespoke suits, and thousand-dollar haircuts. His money stayed in the bank where it grew, giving him the ability to expand, and to create multiple businesses that ran at the same time. Sanur wasn't pushing towards billionaire status, but with the family money, the trust and properties, he was actually pretty close.

He loved open-air markets and street foods, *souks* with heady spices, alleys where he found unexpected treasures. Those people got his money, not yacht makers and jewelers. The family had its own jewels, ancient and priceless. They had artworks from the dawn of time. What more baubles did he need?

Besides, this woman was more beautiful than them all. Now, if she would only believe the same about herself!

TAKEOVER

They signed the handoff paperwork the next week. Tania now owned fifty-one percent of the company. Sanur had her sit at his desk, and she stared at the pen she used to sign the contract for what seemed like hours before putting it away in the desk.

Sanur had already packed his things, and they had an early-morning conference with the initial employees, the orphans and Lupe, before school and work began. Sanur explained that he had sold fifty-one percent of the company to Tania, and that she would be running the company from now on. He would still be making the buying runs, sometimes with Lupe, sometimes with Tania.

Tania had the original staff come in early and explained that it was becoming increasingly hard with the sheer busyness of the office for Sanur to run his other businesses. Tania told them about the office around the corner, and that everything was going to continue exactly the way that it had been. She confessed that she was worried about growing too fast and leaving customers behind.

Lupe stared at both of them, her mouth hanging open. "How the hell did she come up with the money?"

Sanur leaned back against a desk. "Important question, and none of your business, but if you must know, I've sold her over half my shares because I simply do not have the time to devote to this company. I started it because I cared about the artists, their families, the entire communities that get better one person at a time. We're not miracle workers who can cure all of the sick people or make all of the people without legs walk again. But, if people go to bed with full bellies, a roof over their heads, have access to medical care, and are able to send their kids to school, this sickening cycle of poverty doesn't entrap people like quicksand."

"It is impossible that she had the money!" Lupe spat.

Sanur kept his voice calm. "Tania could have purchased the business a month ago. The paperwork was ready. But she owed money and she made sure the entire amount was paid off. And, she has been doing approximately eight jobs around here since I hired her, and being paid for one. We tried paying by the job, but since she was doing them on a daily basis, she still wasn't being compensated correctly. Tania doesn't have the time to do all those jobs anymore, and those of you that want one of her jobs, and the salary she was making for one, can do so."

"In other words, Sanur owed me money." Tania grinned, determined not to get angry with Lupe's tone. "Lupe, you will get a bonus of three thousand euros immediately for working at least two jobs. My suggestion is that you and I work with our young friends here, give them increases in pay in exchange for what they do, or for what we want them to do. Absolutely no one here is just a receptionist, photographer, stager, or customer service representative. You all do multiple jobs. And now Sanur won't be doing jobs around here, and we don't have to pay him."

Tania waited while everyone laughed. "We can use that money to figure out what jobs to pay for and how we want to do that. Do you want to be paid by line item? I was, but it was nowhere close to the actual work I was doing. So, I'm thinking it's a bit more fair to be paid more of a salary, not having to keep track of how many of this or that you do and what rate of pay it is for each one. But, that's up to you if you want to do that much work."

Everyone groaned at doing more work. "Or, you can be paid in percentages of the gross, which may end up being more money. Just understand we're going to have good months and bad months. The bad month thing hasn't happened yet, but it will. Our trajectory has been ever upward. But there is going to be a correction. This can't last forever."

"What about ownership of the business?" asked Lupe.

Sanur shook his head. "You must be out of debt to buy your half, Lupe. Tania has set a good precedence. The rest of you can obtain percentages of the company from these two, if you really feel this is something you want to do. You're young, and you may want to make changes in your lives later on. If you leave, you must sell back your ownership percentages. I won't have people who aren't here on a daily basis making decisions about the company, and neither will Tania. It's too easy to get far away and distracted and not pay attention to what's going on. That's what has been happening to me. I believe in all of you, and in what you can do. This is why I must step aside. But, never worry. I'll be very close by, literally around the corner, because I don't believe in abandoning what I've started."

"We're not even eighteen yet, and you're willing to let us have some percentage of this company?" asked Kannika.

Tania waggled her hand. "Well, you'll have to take percentages of the gross until then. So I suggest you start saving your money from your percentages and your pay increases. You also need to be absolutely certain that this is what you want to do. I'm very sorry to ask this of you, because this means you're making a life decision very early."

Tania leveled a stare at each of them in turn. "Also, you may wish to go to college. Owning part of the company means you get that percentage of the profits, which may actually pay for your university education. But you may also determine after getting your education, whether by university or certificates or whatever it is you choose to do, that you want to get out of this business. In which case, you would have to sell back your percentage of the business." Everyone nodded. "We aren't going to be selling common stock. That means that you can't be some person walking down the street and be a part of this company. This is a family. In case you haven't figured it out, family isn't always blood. It's the people that you trust and love. We are a family; we will continue as a family."

Tania took a breath, kept talking around the lump in her throat. "Sanur will be working on other projects that are just as valuable and important as what we do. One of his businesses is housing people in the worst slums in the world. I think that's important, don't you?"

Aat laughed out loud. "So, you're our mother, Sanur is our father, you two are getting a bit of a divorce, and he's moving around the corner, and Lupe is Auntie?"

Tania threw up her hands. "Why the hell not?" she said, making everyone laugh again. "Actually, I've been looking into it. The thing is, all of you have had to act like adults and make your own decisions here. You've had to grow up far faster than most people do." She got choked up, stared off to the side.

Sanur smiled as those who had figured out what she was talking about stared at her in shock. He'd only been able to take her out on two dates, because he was setting up shipping on multiple continents, looking in on his various projects. Dinner had included talking shop against his own rules and dancing. And kisses. Ones that Tania said "curled her toes." He'd started a new project in Cambodia, and that one needed very careful watching. But he was willing to be distracted by the woman he took out to dinner, the woman who went dancing, her hips swaying to his, those intoxicating kisses that tasted like Coke and dark berries. Tania entranced him with her body, her whirling mind, and her willingness to look after her people. *Our people*, he thought. It was good to have people again, not just employees.

Sanur nodded. "Please be patient, because this will take quite a bit of time. Also, it must not influence your decision to stay here, to go to college, or to decide this is not what you want to do. This is very hard work. It takes an exceptional eye. Customer service becomes very complex because art is in the eye of the beholder. We have clients all over the world. You may end up scattered to the winds if you decide to open offices in other parts of the world."

Aat, moving like a graceful cat, walked up to Sanur and bowed his head. "*Por*," he said, the Thai word for father. Sanur clasped his hands, and Aat bowed over them. Aat then went to Tania, and said, "*Mee*," the Thai word for mother. Tania held out her hands, and he clasped them and bowed over them. Aat then did the same thing with Lupe, and called her "*Aa*," thereby naming Lupe Tania's younger sister, and therefore, his aunt.

Tania let the tears run down her face as each of the orphans called her this. She hugged all of them, wiped the tears away, and said, "This calls for a very short celebration. Let's have our mangoes and juice, and then those calls are going to start coming in. I'm not usually up this early, so I'm probably going to mess something up." She laughed through her tears, and they surrounded her, gave her a group hug.

"What just happened?" asked Lupe in a hushed voice.

"We just did something verbally we haven't yet done legally," Sanur whispered into her ear. "I am going to adopt these children legally." He sighed. "That means we're going to have to work extra hard, because I insist on my children attending at least some university courses. If they're going to take over this business, or any of my other ones, they have to be fully educated."

Lupe stared at him, wide-eyed. "And what did they call me? I know some Thai, but I think they called me a word for 'aunt'."

"Actually, it's a little more complicated than that. You are now officially Tania's younger sister, and an aunt to these young people. Just so you know, this is going to take a while. It will be much easier if...things go as I hope."

Lupe's face grew stony. "I knew you were dating her, but marriage? Does she know that you want to marry her? I also get why you would want to leave the company if you're dating someone who used to be your employee. I didn't think you were one of those nasty men who would treat a woman with such disrespect."

They both accepted plates of mango and orange juice spiked with fizzy water, a poor person's mimosa. "I will never disrespect her. And do you really think she would allow such behavior? To put it bluntly, she would remove my balls if I ever hurt her." Lupe laughed, and like a rubber band snapping back in place, their world returned to normal.

Well, almost normal. Those that had school in the morning took a quick detour to see Sanur's new office. It had the same courtyard with the same pond with nearly identical koi swimming in the pond, a matching bridge over the water, and a cloned reception desk. Inside, there were two separate offices, and only two desks downstairs. There was a small cafe on the bottom right, a convenience store to the left, a dry cleaners in the back left corner, a small Thai kickboxing gym in the back right corner. The only thing missing was a restaurant, and there were five of them surrounding the building, and enough street food to feed everyone three times over.

Everyone took turns seeing the office, helping Sanur move, and then Lawan, an orphan and intern with wide eyes, graceful movements, and a gentle smile, took over as Sanur's receptionist. Sanur already had scripts ready to go and began training her immediately.

$\sim$

Tania entered Sanur's office, a smile on her face. "Hi."

"Hello." Sanur smiled a slow smile, as he shut his laptop and locked it away. "Lawan has already forwarded the phones. There is a cart we haven't tried."

Tania laughed. "Really? I thought we got them all!"

"Other direction. Her pad thai is incredible."

"Then, let's go." They walked, arm in arm. Tania could smell the lime and peanuts from down the street. "This is heavenly."

Sanur laughed. "You haven't tasted anything yet!"

Tania smiled. "I will, trust me."

While they ate, for once Tania followed Sanur's no-work rule. They talked about nothing—last night's rain, a new band that opened for Tania's band, a new outfit Tania bought to strut in onstage. "I'd like to see you in it." He kissed her fingers.

"Tomorrow night," she promised. "Want to see a movie?"

"That would be...excellent." Her movie choices perplexed Sanur. *Pretty in Pink* would follow *Avengers*, then *Four Weddings and a Funeral*, then *Terminator* or *Avatar*. He never complained; he had a beautiful woman in his arms. She would explain the unexplainable to him, he would fail to understand all the nuances, and she would eat popcorn and drink colas and yell at the screen. He found it all...entrancing. Strange, but entrancing.

Tania smiled at him, and his heart stopped when a delivery driver nearly struck her. He had her up and off her chair, protected her with his body. Tania leaned into Sanur, flipped the driver off, said a few choice words. Then, she sat as if she were a queen and ate the rest of her pad thai, wielding chopsticks as if she'd grown up using them.

They stood and paid. She kissed him on the cheek—he still hated public displays of affection during work hours. "Gotta run, new girl to train. See you after work." Sanur knew she was checking out his ass when he left her. It made him feel things he hadn't thought he could feel again. It was exhilarating.

∼

They all met up for lunch. Over a pad thai and various soups, Sanur said to Lawan, "Coordination of the buildings is done onsite with the building manager, and they hire subcontractors. There's also a fixer onsite. It's a fixer's job to prevent corruption. People come around demanding bribes, protection payments, all sorts of things, and if not paid, it will cause trouble and even damage at the site, maybe even block what we are trying to do."

"That's horrific," said Lupe.

Sanur nodded. "I travel so much partly because I must check in with the fixers, make sure everything is going according to plan."

Tania nodded. "Sanur told me about this. Sometimes they want bribes, sometimes they want a room in the new place. Every room for a corrupt official or gang member means one less room for the poor people who actually need it."

Sanur took a sip of mint tea then continued. "There are also constant scammers with substandard building materials, everything from concrete to lumber. They tell themselves false things, such as, 'Why should I spend good money on good products, for people who were just going to tag the walls and live in filth?' They don't care that this building could kill children if it collapses," Sanur said, his voice cold.

Tania's face grew grim. "I happen to know contractors back home from working summers on job sites for money. In the winter, they don't have a hell of a lot to do. I told some of them about what was happening and said that they can make good money overseeing the sites. Some of them are ex-military and work rebuilding houses after hurricanes and tornadoes and that sort of thing."

"So that's why I will talk to someone named Billie Jo today," said Lawan. "She asked to speak to me since I work for Sanur."

"That reminds me," said Sanur. "Billie Jo said to tell you, Tania, that everything was on time and under budget in Indonesia."

"That would be Frank and Bobby," said Tania. "Those boys grew up together, and they doubled in size somewhere between middle and high school. Met them when I volunteered with Habitat for Humanity. They work construction but in the winter they couldn't pay the bills. They tried working on cars, shoveling snow, but that just doesn't fill up the belly, and their momma got sick. They joined the military right after high school and learned construction from the Army."

"They are excellent workers," said Sanur.

"They got all sorts of guys working for them, in the same can't-find-a-job boat come winter. They can go to places like Florida, Phoenix, Las Vegas, someplace hot in the winter, or at least not bitterly cold. Sometimes they find work, sometimes they don't. So they were eager to work for Sanur."

Sanur grinned. "Bobby sent me an e-mail, says he's got little boys and girls onsite from the slums. He uses Foundation money to send the kids to school."

"What foundation?" asked Lupe.

"That's another one of my projects," said Sanur. "I have to displace people to build onsite, unless it's an already crumbled building. Those people get other places to live that are temporary who don't have anyone else to move in with. Their kids go to school, and the able-bodied adults work onsite if they don't already have jobs."

"That's amazing," said Lupe.

"The local schools get scholarships to send every child in an area that wants to go to school. They have to hire local kids to walk the little ones to school or buy vans or buses to pick them up. The kids get free uniforms and backpacks full of school supplies. The parents that don't have jobs work onsite, or as the van and bus drivers, or walk the kids to school, become crossing guards at major streets. Many of these places don't have crossing guards, have never heard of them. People are really proud to get that job, to be protecting children every day. The locals seem to like it too, despite having to stop for the signs."

"You never stop thinking of ways to help people who need it," said Lupe.

Tania narrowed her eyes at him. "You have a medical foundation too, don't you?"

Sanur nodded. "The problem is a sheer lack of doctors and nurses in many areas. In some places, there's only one doctor or nurse for thousands, even hundreds of thousands of people. You can't just send anyone in the world to medical school, either. The person has to be able to handle blood, guts, and pain, and I have to use my funds or to find scholarship money to send local people to medical school."

"Just send an email to Frank, Bobby, and Billie Jo," said Tania. "There have got to be ex-military people who would love to help with recruiting for stuff like that. There has to be some way of sorting through, finding people who want to do this. And I'll make you a bet, it's going to be the women. Provide scholarships and I guarantee they'll be lining up. They may have even had some schooling, they just need to finish."

"I love your mind," said Sanur, placing his palms on both sides of

her head and smiling at her. "So quick, always ready for new ideas."
He let her go, squeezed her fingers, then kissed the tips.

"Father and Mother love each other," said Aat in Thai. Everyone
laughed, then the students went off to school, and everyone else went
back to their offices. Tania didn't see Lupe's face, the flash of venom.
Sanur did.

REVELATION

The beat was in their blood, on their skin. Tania moved under his hands, hips swaying. Sanur had enough. He had a woman, and he needed to see all of her, not glimpses. Sweat on their bodies from dancing in another way. He put his hand on the back of her neck, kissed her deeply. She groaned, grabbed his hand, and pulled him out into the night. They went back to her place on his bike. Feeling the vibration between his legs made him insane. He needed, wanted, desired so much more.

Sanur put the helmets away, and Tania led him, keycard by keycard, into her apartment. He shut the door with his foot, then found himself up against it. He felt those small hands slide over his skin. He carefully slid off his shirt, rolled it up, and threw it on her kitchen chair. She did the same with her own spaghetti-strap golden top. He slid his fingers over her breasts, kissed her throat, nibbled her ear sharply. She moaned, slid her hands ever downward.

He gasped as she reached into his slacks, undid them. He kicked off his shoes, stepped out of the slacks. It was not in his nature to kick them aside, so he just left them there, stepped to the right. She lifted one foot, then another. Her sandals went flying, then her golden lace camisole bra. Her breasts were swollen, tight.

Sanur knelt, licked with gentle flicks, sucked. Prayed to his goddess. Tania gasped, moaned, ran her fingers through his hair. She stepped out of her crimson skirt, threw it on the same chair where his shirt lay in a crumpled ball. He slid his fingers downward, ever downward. Tania gasped, hitched her breath, moaned, and then threw her head back. Her whole body clenched, released.

Sanur rejoiced. He had found the right way to please her. He stepped back to another chair, brought her with him, hands on her hips. He slid off her bikini underwear, left his own boxers on. It was time for him to worship her. He slid his fingers down, slid his fingers into her honey. She sat, legs suddenly boneless.

He knelt, kissed her, slid down her neck, kissed those perfect breasts again with flicks of his tongue. She hissed, arched her back again, and gasped. He kissed lower and lower, and she clawed his hair, stroked his cheek, slid her hands down his arms.

He opened her legs wide, kissed the inside of each thigh. He used the tip of his long tongue to make her gasp again and again. She mewled, gasped harder and harder, and mewled again, arched her back, and groaned. Finally, limp in his arms, she said, "Bed." He stood, picked her up, and carried her to bed. Staggered, righted himself. He felt her lay her head on his chest. *"Rani.* My queen." She felt so strong under his hands. He stood her up, pulled back the sheets, slid her into them. He knelt, helped her relax on the pillow.

And then, his phone went off. He seriously considered throwing it out the window. He answered it. A terrified man began speaking in the Old Language about lions. It was one of Supayalat's people, sent to set up motorcycle pathways to get the goods to market. Security was missing and part of the road was damaged. Someone had called the police. He sighed, and said, "I wish to speak to the lion."

He mouthed, *I must go.* Tania waved a hand. Her hair was spread out against the pillow. He longed to make her comfortable. He went into the bathroom, put warm water on a washcloth for her.

A growly voice came on the line. "We know the situation. Who called the police?"

"I do not know. We will pay the hyenas, but we want safety for our road and our people. They carry the products of the people in your area. If they prosper, so you do as well." He crossed back to the bedroom, pulled back the sheet, cleaned his love's trembling body, and pulled the covers back over her. Sanur sighed as the lion roared. He would have to go to Zimbabwe to solve the problem. He put the cloth away in the hamper, kissed her lips. She sighed, rolled over, already sliding into sleep.

Sanur dressed while he soothed and cajoled using some very ancient protocols and agreements, and then was out the door. Lawan would find him a flight, get him to where he could solve the problem. He winced, wondered when he would have time with his woman again.

~

Supayalat met him at the airport. "It is resolved?"

Sanur hissed. "Yes. I had to hire more pride people to supervise the hyenas." He turned slitted eyes towards her. "I need for you to deal with this. I need time with my woman."

"How is Htay?"

"She is well. Her doctor says things are well."

"You must tell your woman all things."

Sanur hissed out a sigh. "You are correct."

Supayalat relaxed. She had not expected the capitulation. "She will be shocked. Surprised. She may not react the way you expect."

Sanur grinned. "I think she is strong enough. Her reaction may surprise you."

Supayalat hissed. "I hope you are right."

~

Tania came back from lunch with Sanur, back from his weeklong trip. She was grinning, thinking of pairing *Breakfast Club* with an episode of *The Stand*. She enjoyed confusing him. Tania hadn't had access to much except for her cousin's very old '80s movies still on VHS. So she knew a lot more of that decade than she should.

Tania thought of his hands on her neck, sliding ever downward. His kisses down her neck. Sliding into bed and, frustratingly, the phone call just when she had been ready for so much more. Tania sighed, thinking the best idea would be to skip the movie. She opened the door to the office and stepped inside, smiling at the caress of cool air on her skin.

Lupe met her at the door. "Nice of you to join us."

Tania tilted her head. "I'm actually early. Is there a problem?"

"Well, if you think losing a client is bad."

"What seems to be the problem?" Tania headed towards her office. There were staff members still on the phone. Splitting the lunches was a good idea; more customers were helped, and the interns loved having transition time between work and school.

"The African line."

Tania nodded her head and opened her office door. Ever since Tania had taken over, Lupe seemed to find the African line personally offensive. "What seems to be the problem?" she asked again.

"A customer put in a large order, and it's shipping out at separate times."

Tania raised her eyebrows. "If it's the Caberos account, I specifically told her that would be the case. They are making her order by hand. Is it?"

"Well, yes."

"Did she specifically call to complain?"

Lupe tapped her foot. "No, I was looking through the invoices and saw the delay."

Tania went behind her desk and sat down. "The African line is mine. I know I told you to approach me if you have any questions, but this isn't your job. The African line is my job. Auditing my work is not your job, Lupe. Please stick to your own work."

Lupe made a face. "I'm trying to help you."

Tania shook her head. "I also don't want to hear one more word criticizing the African line. You have your own lines. Please work on that."

"I can't help you if you reject my input." Lupe stomped her foot like a child.

"I am your boss, Lupe. Stomping your foot is childish. Trying to help your boss with something she has told you not to touch is also unprofessional. Now, do you have anything else to say to me?" Tania kept her voice soft, smooth like butter. Lupe was complaining nearly every day, wasting everyone's time.

"No."

"Okay, then, it's lunchtime for you. I tried a food cart with Sanur going to the left, not the right. You might like it."

Lupe rolled her eyes. "I'll get my own food, thank you."

Tania tilted her head, gave a little wave. "See you later, then!" Lupe shut the door. Tania took a deep breath. *Who turned on her snark?* she wondered.

~

Tania decided to pick up Sanur at his new office. The air was wet and heavy. She stood outside his office as he completed a phone call while he closed his laptop and put it away in a locked drawer. Sanur turned off the lights in the office with the other hand and walked out to the front desk. He turned off the rest of the lights, pulled down the security door, and locked it.

Tania wore a flowy pale blue top with a deep blue skirt, silver and blue sandals, and a smile. Sanur looked cool and breezy in khakis and a silvery shirt. They went to the koi pond and threw food for the fish. "They are so beautiful, gold, white, and silver." Tania smiled.

"I like having them nearby."

She brushed his coppery-black hair out of his eyes. "I need to get the dye lot for this color. It's prismatic dye, absolutely gorgeous."

Sanur laughed, then took both her hands and his. "Have I ever lied to you?" Sanur looked into her eyes.

"No, because if you did, I would quit, then kick your ass, and you would never see me again."

He laughed. "Good to know. I'm telling the absolute truth when I tell you that I do not dye my hair. My mother's hair had a golden sheen, and my father's had copper."

Tania quieted at the talk of his parents. She knew they had been dead for many years, and from experience that losing both parents must hurt. "Do you have pictures of them?"

"My people were very reticent about having their picture taken. But I do have some pictures in my home. I will show you sometime." He bent down and kissed her. He felt the tingling everywhere, from her hands on both sides of his face, from his lips touching hers, from the intimacy of the moment. He was able to compartmentalize, run businesses and foundations with moving and intersecting parts all over the world that didn't have any right to be solvent yet somehow were. Yet, he found himself completely unable to think when that wash of electric warmth rolled over him.

Sanur kissed her again and again, and the world fell away once again, the fish surfacing for their pellets, the moist heat against his body after the rains. He pulled back so he could see her, the lowered sun's fading light striking her shoulders so that her skin seemed translucent. The look in her eyes when she saw him, how a light appeared behind them that made her seem to glow, made him want to wrap himself around her. He dove in again.

He lost himself in her until she took her hands away from his face and smiled up at him. "This is wonderful. But I'm hungry!"

"My majordomo is making dinner, a chicken dish I think you will enjoy. Would you like to come with me to dinner?"

"I would be honored." She bowed her head a little.

Sanur's heart quickened with anticipation. They had both been ready for some time, but the sale of the business came first. He would not be that man, the one that disrespected women. He saw it all around him, how hungry eyes saw people as objects or paychecks. But now, nothing was in his way. Tania thrummed in his veins, under his skin. He would have waited an eternity for her.

She took his hand, waiting on him to lead her to his home. He closed the fish food box, pulled out his phone, then sent a quick text, *Two for dinner.* He had to look long and hard to find a program that had that particular font. The language was very old, spoken when the world was young.

The reply came quickly. *She honors us.*

They took a *tuk tuk* because a lightly spitting rain began to fall, and they were soon out of the city into the countryside. Traditional Thai homes were built on stilts above the ground because of flooding. They were wooden with pointed roofs. Sanur's home had steps leading up to the ground floor, and had a porch wrapped around the house. The wooden house was stained a deep red, boxes filled with delicate pink and purple orchids, and fragrant white jasmine. The property stretched back, palm trees surrounding the house. Tania scrambled out, delighted. Sanur paid the *tuk tuk* driver, and he drove away.

There was a pond in front, and Tania was pleased to find koi swimming inside. She fed them handfuls of fish food she found in its box on a wooden pole, like he had at work. They came to her, golden and white bodies churning, mouths open. There was a small van parked on the left side under the house. Tania figured it was trans-portation for Htet, the majordomo.

They took off their shoes at the base of the stairs. There was a bench on the landing, in case someone got exhausted going up the stairs. The railings had beautiful decorations on them, and she touched the carvings. "I take it you got an artist to carve these?" He smiled and nodded.

There was another bench at the top and double doors opening up. There were lime trees in pots on either side of the door. Inside, there were beautiful wooden floors that glowed under the light. There was a window that looked over the side. There was a door that led into the main room with a comfortable couch, in a deep coppery color with black and gold pillows, and a flat-screen TV hung on the back wall.

They went through a door on the right and went over to an open walkway that led to the kitchen. The kitchen was in chrome and black, with modern appliances that seemed to be smaller than normal. The cooking surface was on a kitchen island.

Htet looked like an older version of Sanur, tall and thin, with a flat face and mahogany skin. He kept his black hair cut very short. Htet was sizzling something in a silver pan. There was a green salad and three small bowls on the wooden dining table with four carved wooden chairs with cushioned seats around it. Sanur rushed to wash his hands, then he poured oil, vinegar, and lime juice into a little bowl and mixed it up with the tiny whisk. "Tania, this is Htet, my majordomo. He runs the house, the lands, and many of my other affairs for me. Htet, this is Tania. Tania, please sit back and relax."

"The chicken is almost done," said Htet. The smells of ginger, garlic, soy sauce, and lime were heavenly. Tania washed her hands, then sat at the kitchen table to watch the action. Htet slid the chicken out of the frying pan and onto a plate, turned off the heat, and immediately washed and wiped out the frying pan. Sanur took over and shredded the chicken with two forks. A bowl of vegetables was already on the counter, and Tania could see and smell garlic, ginger, green onions, and mushrooms.

Sanur deftly added the chicken, vegetables, some chopped boiled egg, and vinaigrette to the salad, then tossed it. The majordomo returned to slice some French bread, and Sanur pressed baked garlic with a fork into a small bowl. He added freshly grated ginger, balsamic vinegar, olive oil, and a touch of honey in a little bowl and mixed them.

Htet brought the food to the table, then the majordomo came over with three cans of Coke and gorgeous crystal glasses with ice. "The ice is made from filtered water. No one drinks tap water here."

The men surrounded the table, standing behind their chairs. Tania had the presence of mind to stand up as well and stand behind her chair. They put their hands together and bowed their heads, and so did she. They spoke in a language she didn't understand, one with hisses and clicks and a lot of complex vowel sounds. They lifted their heads, smiled, and sat down. Tania followed suit.

They ate the delicious chicken salad, and Sanur taught Tania how to dunk the bread in the vinaigrette and use it to eat the salad. They used forks and chopsticks that looked to be pure silver, heavy, with an intricate pattern. The two men spoke in English, and the majordomo flashed a beautiful smile when he heard that the teens wanted to be adopted. "That sounds absolutely wonderful," he said, clapping his hands together. "I will call Tran about the paperwork. The trust fund is already set up per your instructions, *Veera*."

Tania narrowed her eyes. "How long have you been planning to adopt them?" She sipped her Coke.

"Ever since you brought them to work for us," said Sanur. "But you keep bringing more in, so the paperwork gets a little more complicated each time."

Tania let her jaw drop. "Every single time I brought someone from the orphanage to work for us, you planned to adopt them?"

Sanur shrugged. "No one else will make sure that they are provided for. That is my responsibility."

"Most employers wouldn't do such a thing. I was going to do it after I paid you off for half the company. Actually, I was going to do it when I finished paying off my debts and could figure out how much I needed to pay a lawyer. Then you offered for me to buy half the company. I hadn't sought out the lawyer yet."

The majordomo glanced over at Sanur. He bowed his head, and said, "You have chosen well, *Veera*."

Tania blushed. "Thank you, Htet. Vera is a woman's name in the United States, but I doubt that's what you're trying to call him."

Sanur laughed. "Perceptive," he said. "The term is *veera*, in ancient Sanskrit a name for 'brave' or 'courageous,' often referring to royalty. In ancient times, my family served and sometimes became royalty themselves, from what was once Burma, all the way down to India, over to Thailand and Cambodia in the time of the Khmer, the old kingdom. Our ways have followed us through the centuries, the responsibility for others, the desire to make the world a better place, to make the world safer."

Tania listened closely, wide-eyed. Sanur pointed a piece of bread at Tania as he spoke. "Times of strife killed our people, no matter where they were located. We had to spread out to keep ourselves alive. There is always greed, hunger for what you do not have. We worked very hard to build ourselves up to be of maximum service to others."

Sanur ate his bread, and Htet took over the narrative. "The arrival of Siddhartha Buddha cemented our thoughts, gave a mechanism for our most ancient beliefs. Sadly, we do not know from whence we came. The story of our origins is lost in the mists of time. We have had to rebuild so many times, century after century. So much vanished."

Sanur nodded. "But servants such as Htet have given us great continuity, the ability to trace ourselves back to the servants of kings, even to the kings and queens themselves. We have done our best to rule benevolently, to maximize the peace in the middle of suffering. Women were equal to men thousands of years ago in our family's culture." He reached out, touched Tania's hand. "Finding you, that has been something I never thought to find."

They finished their dinner, talked about less consequential things. Htet stood to clean off the table, for they had eaten everything. "That was one of the most delicious meals I've ever had. It was simple, elegant, and perfect." Tania rubbed her stomach.

"Thank you very much," said Htet. "Simple food is often the best." He inclined his head, stacked up the dishes, and took them to the sink to be washed.

"Can I help with something?" Tania asked.

Sanur chuckled out a laugh. "He would be highly offended if you did. He only lets me help with the cooking because I insist. I enjoy it from time to time." He held her hand and drew her from the kitchen and dining area. "Come. I have something to show you."

Sanur took the walkway to the left, and they went behind the house to another building on stilts. "How big is this thing?" asked Tania.

"Htet sleeps in a bedroom over the carport. The man deserves his privacy after all he does for me. I am bringing you into my private space."

Sanur opened the intricately carved wooden door, and she stepped inside. The bed was huge, covered by mosquito netting, with white sheets and pillowcases, and a light coppery cover on top. Tapestries hung on the walls next to the bed on the right.

What she saw out of her left eye stunned her. In wooden boxes behind glass were the shed skins of a snake with a white underbelly, golden and white, with a coppery head. They ranged in size from tiny to one that took over nearly the entire left wall. She strode over to the smallest one, and said, "A golden python? Where is it?"

"It's very close by, but do not be afraid. This python eats a chicken once a week and was fed two days ago. It is very intelligent and friendly, and it loves you."

"I'm not afraid of snakes. The corn snakes protect the crops, the garden ones are very small and wouldn't hurt anyone. If you've got a golden python that eats a chicken, and not me, that's perfectly fine. But how would a snake, who never met me, love me?" Tania asked.

"I have something to show you. There is a secret that I must maintain. I believe you are strong enough to find out the secret. If you find out and then want to leave, please go talk to Htet. He will call you a *tuk tuk*, and you can go home. The businesses are now separated, and so you never have to see me again if you don't want to."

"Now you're just trying to scare me, and I don't scare easily. What the hell are you talking about?" Tania was getting angry, and Sanur knew it was time. He closed his eyes, then opened them to take off his clothes. He folded them, piled them on the bed, then stepped back. Tania raised her eyebrows and smiled a little looking at his naked body. He let the magic, the golden light, flow over him, felt himself change. Soon, he was a two-and-a-half meter long golden Burmese python with a coppery head.

Tania let her jaw drop, and a half-scream came out. She hyperventilated for a moment and stepped towards the bed. "My man is...a snake," she said, her voice strangled. She leaned her calves against the silky coverlet and breathed in and out. She unclenched her hands, then stood upright as the man-snake made no move towards her. She knew she would have to go to him.

Even in a snake form, Sanur still felt the consciousness of the man. But now he had a snake's eyes and had to use his tongue to smell her. She stepped towards the bed, then didn't move for a very long time. Then she lowered herself, very slowly. He rose, very slowly raising his head. She touched his head, and he tasted only a hint of fear from the air. She was a very strong, tough woman, and there was a possibility she would attack. But she did not. She reached under him and lifted him with a grunt. He lay on her shoulders, entwined around her, took in her heat, wound himself into her hair.

Htet kept him on a one-chicken-a-week diet because he didn't want to turn into something so large that his future wife, whether she be human or shapeshifter, would be unable to carry him. He also didn't want to crave larger and larger prey.

Tania stood under his weight, her arms straining. Sanur wound himself more tightly in her hair. Tania took one step forward, then the next. She felt so sensuous and warm next to his skin. He decided to let her do whatever she wanted, and she opened the door and walked across the bridge, slowly, without staggering. She opened the door to the kitchen and inclined her head at Htet. Htet moved as well, but his snake sight couldn't tell exactly what Htet did, only the movement itself, probably a bow. Sanur approved of Htet's calm scent.

Tania stepped backwards, closed the kitchen door, turned around, and slowly walked back to the bedroom. She closed the door behind her, knelt, and Sanur slithered to the ground.

The magic usually didn't let him shift quickly from one body to another, but somehow he knew it would work because he loved her. He rose as high as he could under his own weight, and she touched his head. He lowered himself and willed back his human body. The magic allowed him to turn back into a man, and he lowered his head, thanking the Goddess for allowing this quick transformation from man to snake and back again. He took his time standing up, completely naked.

Tania took one breath, then another. She said quietly, "In America, we use lines in a doorway or on a wall to tell how quickly children grow. We usually don't save shed skin. But it works for this particular problem." She reached out and stroked his face, as Sanur rose to face her. "So you've been able to do this since you were an infant?"

Sanur laughed. "Golden pythons are born from eggs, as many as fifty of them, in the wild. Our mothers give birth only in human form and only have one or two children, because human bodies are not built to carry fifty babies. Very early in our existence, after having fought to survive, changing into a very weak human baby would have killed us. Imagine having to take care of fifty human infants at once! I think that's why the magic works the other way, allowing us to be born in the human way. But, around age five we begin to change, and by six or so we move back and forth until we have the power to choose."

"I thought shapeshifters didn't become able to shift until their teens." Tania laughed at herself, a little wildly. "Wait, that's movies." Her eyes were luminous, her skin pale, her breathing a little ragged, the only sign she had just carried her lover around her neck and in her hair as a snake.

Sanur wrapped a copper sarong around himself and sat down on the bed. Tania sat down next to him. "One of many things pop culture gets wrong. And our parents were made in the human way and have human children."

She stroked her fingers down his hand, relieved. "Good."

Sanur smiled gently. "In the past, we were sent out to live in multiple households, learn as many ways of life and as many skills as possible. This was called fostering in Europe, a way of life with us. This is why I was not as destroyed at my parents' deaths that you may consider me to be. My father left when I was small. My mother left me with a couple in order to find him, and they died in a *tuk tuk* accident. What was destructive was my ending up with improper parents." He pointed to a silver frame, partly hidden by a book. Tanya looked around the book to see a woman's face. She had Sanur's eyes and his nose and beautiful smile and hair tinged with gold. Ethereal, otherworldly. Next to that picture was a much smaller photo of a man with Sanur's high forehead, strong jaw, and copper hair. Obviously the father.

Tania nodded. "The couple was paid to raise you, then put you in an orphanage. Then Htet found you."

Sanur nodded. "Htet found me again and sent me to boarding schools. I made friends with some boys who became my brothers. They helped slip me out of the orphanage when I needed to become a python."

Tania tilted her head. "The friend who fell in love with your woman, and they stole your money and left. Did that guy know?"

Sanur shook his head. "No. I am so very glad he did not. But if he had, I doubt he would have behaved the way he did. I think...I think he would have been afraid of me. Too afraid to do what he has done."

Tania began by taking off her skirt, then her blouse, carefully folding them up. "Were any of these people you considered family shapeshifters?"

"No. I have only met a few, various branches of the family. They are all over the world, not just Asia. My kind only lives in those countries where it would seem to be normal to keep a python as a pet."

Tania laughed, a little wobbly. "So I can introduce you to my friends twice, once as my boyfriend, once as my giant pet python I somehow managed to smuggle into the country."

Tania stood up, walked over, looked down at Sanur. He stood, and she looked him in the eye. "My life has been a series of bizarre events. I guess this is why I seem to be so calm now." Her voice shook. "What am I saying? This is so weird." She held out her shaking hands; Sanur took her hands in his. "I let you take your time with me, believing you were nervous about my past. But you were holding back because of who you were. I find that a little bit...amazing. Back in my small town, everybody knew. Couldn't get a guy to touch me with a ten-foot pole, unless he thought I was a whore. Had a few guys in college, not from my hometown, obviously. Tried it with a girl, but I preferred men."

Sanur snorted. Tania grinned. "A few guys in college. So, I've done the deed completely normally. You don't have to worry about hurting me, giving me some sort of flashback or making me feel bad. I like sex, I enjoy it. I just don't have it with anyone that walks by. I wanted to be with someone who's worth it. And even though you turn into a snake, everything about you says to me that you are respectful, loving, and kind."

She kissed each of his thumbs, then gently kissed him. "We have this electroshock thing going on. When I touch you it feels like electricity. It may be your magic, your shape-shifting ability. The fact that you're partly human and partly something else is just...a part of you. Disturbing, but interesting. I just don't want it to stop." Her voice went breathy, trailed off.

"Neither do I." Sanur kissed her forehead, her nose, both cheeks, her mouth. He took his time, tasting her dark berry cola lips, then just held her close for the longest time. He had to let go, because another part of his anatomy let him know rather clearly than he needed to move this along. He helped her out of her camisole with its shelf bra and her panties, both in a cobalt blue that stood out against her skin.

Sanur led her to the bed, took off his sarong and threw it on the end of the bed, took a box of condoms out of the dresser drawer and ripped it open. She laughed. "Good, because I really didn't want to deal with fifty babies quite at the moment." He grunted laughter and stole her breath with a kiss. He kissed her neck, stroked her shoulders, stroked lines down her back with the tips of his fingers, making her shudder. "I'm glad you came to the party ready."

She kissed his neck, nibbled on an earlobe. He groaned, pushed her onto the bed, and started kissing his way down her neck. Sanur tasted her hot sweetness and wondered what he had done to deserve his equal coming into his life. "*Rani*," he called her, the Sanskrit word for queen. They kissed for a long time as he stroked her back, ran his fingers through her hair, caressed her face, her neck. He fell, and fell, and was gone.

～

*A*fterward, Sanur moved their clothes at the end of the bed onto the wooden bench on the side of the room, rolled off the now-sodden coppery silken blanket, pulled down the sheets, and slipped her in. He opened the door to the bathroom and slid the blanket into the hamper. He washed his hands and came out to find her grinning at him right outside the bathroom doorway, her red hair tousled.

"My turn." She entered the bathroom and squealed at the double glass sinks and large rain head shower tiled in copper. There was also a granite tub on the other side, more of a soaking bath to sit in, like a spa. She shoved him out of the bathroom, did her thing, and came back to slide into bed next to him. It took some time, stroking and licking each other, but soon they were both willing to go again.

They slid into sleep and woke up to rain on the roof. The light in the room was dim, but they could see enough to take one more time to love each other. Sanur held Tania close, felt her slide into sleep again. Soon, exhaustion drew him under with her.

BREAKDOWN

*I*n the morning, they showered together, and Sanur was happy all over again that he had such a large shower built. They were slow with their movements, exhausted. "Was what happened last night...real?" Tania asked, after drying her hair.

Sanur kissed her neck. "Yes, I am really a snake shifter, from a long line of snake shifters. You needed to know what I am." He kissed her nose. "It was time." Sanur dressed in blue underwear, a golden shirt, and blue shorts. He gave her a pair of blue gym shorts and a khaki shirt that was ridiculously loose on her to wear. "We will buy clothes for you today that you can keep here." She put her clothes on, brushed her hair with a brush from her purse, and they walked back to the kitchen.

Htet prepared warm croissants, fruit, and little pots of chocolate along with tea and mango juice for breakfast. Htet gave Tania a tablet computer, open to a website with women's clothing. "Please order whatever you like, *Rani,*" he said to Tania.

Tania took the tablet and lay it on the table. She quickly chose underwear, then ordered some shorts, khaki pants, and tops, then put the tablet down and began eating her food. She looked at first one man, then the other. "*Rani* means queen, doesn't it?" she asked them both.

Htet inclined his head, and Sanur grinned. "She learns things quickly."

"She does," agreed Sanur, sipping his tea. "That she does."

~

Two days later, Tania stood in front of the desks, listening to her people with headsets on, something she liked to do about three times a day. She heard Achara dealing with a customer who was obviously dithering. Since the person spoke English, Tania walked up behind her, tuned into the call with a single button on her headset, and took over the call in a honeyed Southern accent.

The woman was actually from America but lived in Singapore and had very eclectic tastes. Tania formed a picture of the woman in her mind, golden skin, tasteful silver earrings, and most likely burnished golden hair, a shade a stylist had managed to copy from the spun-sugar hair of a child.

"Now, sugar," said Tania, getting into the role. "I see you can't decide between the African mirror and the Balinese one. The African one is more dramatic and should go in your hallway. A woman always needs to check the mirror before she leaves. If you have space for another mirror, such as to reflect the artwork and your beautiful living room, go ahead and get the other one. Why make a choice at all? Just order one this month and one the next month. Problem solved." The woman read off her credit card number, and Tania smiled while Achara put the number into the system and completed the order.

"Some people are ditherers. That means they can't make a decision. Make it for them, but very politely, in a way that they can't see that that's what you're doing."

"Yes, Mom," said Achara. Tania made a face with goo-goo eyes at her, making Achara laugh, and continued her rotation. Lupe was upstairs on a photo shoot, obvious from the sound of furniture moving around over their heads. On the floor, the calls were coming in fast and furious.

The desks were arranged in a circle, and Tania could stand in the middle of them and listen to everything. Tania was fiercely proud of all of them, and she had thoroughly documented her training program so that Kannika and Achara could take on more and more day-to-day training and oversight work, and could handle things if Tania went out of town.

Tania fielded some calls, one of them a Spanish-speaking customer who needed some things shipped rather quickly. The other was a young woman with an art gallery who absolutely loved the idea of having console tables and other things like that which she could sell if she wanted to. "We will surround you with beautiful things. Why don't I send over three or four things? Pay me for them and be sure to tell your customers they're for sale. If they don't sell, we can trade the pieces out, but somehow I doubt that's going to be a problem." The owner of the art gallery wanted a contract, so Tania modified one to cover that situation, emailed it to the woman, and got a signed copy back within ten minutes.

Tania sent the staff an email explaining that designers could choose to do this, but that they had to buy the pieces first. She included a copy of the contract, and asked that the calls be transferred to herself or Lupe if they came in.

Tania was still out on the floor, ready to field a few more calls, when Lupe came up to her, jaw set, face red, obviously spitting mad. Tania flipped her eyes over to her office, but Lupe decided to have a meltdown in front of everybody. "How dare you make a contract like this without speaking to me first?" she screamed directly in Tania's face. "We don't do things on consignment!"

Tania held up a hand. "Please lower your voice. Customers on the phone can hear you. If you had bothered to read the contract, you would see that all of the pieces must be purchased first." Tania kept her voice low, polite, even creamy. Her mother had been a master at not seeing the obvious, at covering over unpleasantness. Tania had learned from the best.

"What do you mean I didn't bother reading the contract? Do you think I'm stupid? Are you calling me *estupido?*" Lupe spat the words into Tania's face.

"Please enter my office. We can talk there." Tania pointed. "Professionals have discussions in offices." Tania let a tiny bit of steel show.

"Fuck you," said Lupe. There was a scrape of chairs as people picked up their laptops and went out into the courtyard, wireless headphones still on their heads. Tania desperately hoped their noise-canceling headphones would cover up Lupe's screaming.

Tania went to the still, quiet place she had gone for many years, the place where nothing could reach her to do harm. "I get that you're upset. But that was the most unprofessional behavior you could have possibly had. Supervisors are in control of their emotions. And right now you aren't in any sort of control, right in the middle of our workplace while people are trying to help customers on the phone." She turned and strode to the office, forcing Lupe to follow.

Once they were in the office, Tania walked behind her desk. "You could have had forty-nine percent of the company. Sanur already had the paperwork drawn up. Apparently, that's not what you want. That's good to know. There are boxes in the storage area. Please clean out your desk." Her voice had lost the buttery tones, but was very calm and polite, and pitched very low so that Lupe had to strain to hear.

"You can't fire me," said Lupe, her voice venomous.

"I own fifty-one percent of this company, so, yes, I can. Please pack your things and leave at once."

"No, you don't." Lupe's voice was shrill. "You had to borrow money from Sanur to buy fifty-one percent of the company! That means that he owns it!"

"No, I borrowed money from a trust. And the percentage I borrowed was relatively small. I've already paid off nearly half. And, I'm done speaking with you. You've done very well here and have been able to accumulate a great deal. By the time your desk has been cleaned off, I should have your contract reviewed and whatever money is owed to you ready to go."

Lupe stared at her. "I thought we were friends." Her voice was an ugly growl in her throat.

"So did I. But your behavior just now was incredibly unprofessional. People have disagreements all the time, personally and professionally. But they don't have them on the customer service floor in front of the employees. A person made a simple purchase, and you decided to blow that completely out of proportion. That person may buy more from us, especially since I believe the pieces she chose will sell. People can buy our things and resell them if they want to. It's kind of how business works. Now, I want you to leave."

"Why the fuck did Sanur choose you to own fifty-one percent of the company?" demanded Lupe, leaning over the desk, trying to get into Tania's personal space.

Tania leaned right back and spoke directly into Lupe's face. "I don't know. You'll have to ask him. Why don't you do that? But I suggest not going in there screaming. I don't think he'll react well to that. If you're looking for a guess, which is all I can offer you, it's that my debt was nearly paid off. I worked very hard and got a very lucky break with an employer who was willing to have a trust loan me the money to pay off my debt faster. Then there's the fact that I was doing about eight jobs, and I got reimbursed for that too."

Tania pitched her voice even lower, got right into Lupe's face. "But, believe me, I would have paid it off, even if I had to live in some of the places I've lived in back home. I lived in a place so tiny that there were three closets, barely big enough to stand up in. One held the few clothes I had, the second held a tiny refrigerator and a hot plate, and the third held a bathroom so small that the door hit the toilet, and you couldn't get in if the shower stall door was open. Have you ever lived like that, Lupe? I have, and I'm not afraid to go back there if it will dig me out of where I was."

Lupe stared at Tania, aghast, silent with shock. "I took on job after job here, learned everything by being thrown in the deep end. I made so many mistakes that I thought Sanur was going to throw me out the window half the time. I ordered the wrong part for the printer and blew the thing up. I aggravated the wrong client. I hung up on people until I understood the phone system. But I learned, and I grew. Is my good fortune an amazing, miraculous turn of events? Hell, yes. But I did work hard. Now, the door is over there."

"You screwed your way into this company, you little *puta*."

Tania fought to not let her jaw drop. "We had one real kiss, in the heat of the moment. A very amazing one, but only one. Sanur ran like hell and decided to wait until my debts were paid off and he had withdrawn from the company to make another move. You can call me a whore all you want. I've been called a hell of a lot worse by people I considered even closer friends, people who knew me from childhood. But, at this point, you're calling Sanur someone who sexually harasses women. He is not, and if he had I would have taken him to a court of law, and I would have removed his face first. He is quite literally the most honest man I've ever known, and I've known some very good people."

Tania put her hands on the desk and leaned forward a little more, her voice very low and biting. "So you can take your petty, jealous bullshit from middle school and shove it up your ass. You have just proven several things to me. First, you cannot handle your emotions. Second, you're quite willing to behave extremely unprofessionally. Third, you're willing to destroy relationships by throwing grenades on them. Fourth, you make unfounded assumptions. If you knew either one of us at all, you would know that simply could not have happened. Now, for the last damn time, pack up your shit and get the hell out of here." She looked over Lupe's shoulder and smiled.

Sanur said from the doorway, "I completely agree." Lupe jumped and whirled around at his silent entry. "Pack your things immediately. I will wire money into your account based on your contract. I never want to see your face again." Lupe whirled, faced Sanur. Tania knew that look on Sanur's face. It was a look of a predator ready to strike. His papery, spicy-incense scent filled the room.

Unfortunately, Lupe still didn't get exactly how much trouble she was in. "How much money I owe is none of your business. I didn't owe you a thing. And yet you delayed selling me half the company? For what? For you to fuck your girlfriend?"

Sanur stepped into the room and shut the door behind him. Sanur's voice took on a very interesting, sinuous timbre. "How would you have gotten the money to buy half the company?" Sanur asked Lupe.

Lupe looked like a cat ready to strike, claw, and spit, but her jaw was clenched shut. Sanur smiled grimly. "You would have asked the people that you call friends. Some of them are wonderful people that I also call friends. Some of them are not, and some of them are quite dangerous. Do you understand that this is a family-owned company? Do you know that I would have offered you slightly under half of a company because I considered you to be part of the family? Those people you would have asked, they had no part in this business. They would have been looking for a quick payout, possibly at a ruinous interest rate that you couldn't possibly afford to pay back. And those people will never own part of anything that I own. I will make sure of it." Sanur slit his eyes. Lupe stared at him, wide-eyed.

Sanur stepped forward, focused unblinking, flat eyes on Lupe's wild ones. "You didn't think about any of that. You just wanted money, and possibly power and prestige. You desired, and then you became jealous, the emotions of a little child. How many times have I explained to you that I will not tolerate your snubs, your cold tone, the way that you have treated Tania since she took over? Instead of stepping up and becoming an adult, you acted like a child. So, I had already put aside that new contract."

Lupe recoiled as Sanur stepped closer. "You haven't thought once of the people you have abandoned upstairs during your photo shoot. You didn't think about all of those workers that had to run out into the courtyard so that their customers wouldn't hear you screaming and cursing. And now you've accused me of a heinous crime. If Tania permitted it, which she most certainly would not. If I hurt her in any way, she would be on the next plane to anywhere other than here, after she physically, mentally, or emotionally damaged me in some way. Now. Get. Out." He stepped aside.

Lupe glared at both of them and barged past Sanur. He caught the door lightning-fast as Lupe tried to slam it, then gently shut it.

"I've read the contract while you were talking to…to her." Tania waved at the screen while working to control her breathing. "It reads exactly the same as my old one. She won't receive anything other than the time until now, and we just got paid. That's not even enough for a plane ticket."

"Someone has been feeding her this nonsense. I have an enemy, someone who wants to take over the company through Lupe. I'll give you two guesses."

"Malee and Somchair. Your friend and his lover that screwed you over before, literally." Sanur snorted. "I ignored Lupe's little barbs over the last few weeks because I figured she would be signing the contract pretty soon and get over it. And because it was too petty to even acknowledge. That was probably a mistake." Tania sighed, then paced a little bit behind her desk. "If she had signed the paperwork to own part of the company, it would have been disastrous. How did I not see that she was so far off the deep end? Am I crazy, blind, or just an idiot?"

"None of the above. This is a plan that has been running underground for some time. You took someone into this company out of the kindness of your heart, then this person decided to listen to the wrong people. Little snubs are a huge jump to what just happened today."

"Point taken. Now, if you'll excuse me, I have a photo shoot to finish, and I suggest that you make sure Little Miss Crazy doesn't run off with all of our accounts or something." She stepped past Sanur, and he gently touched her back.

"I will do as you say." Sanur gave Tania another one of his enigmatic smiles. "But the minute I heard about this little altercation, I blocked her from accessing anything at all."

Sanur followed Tania out of her office. Tania headed upstairs to finish the photo shoot but stayed at the top of the stairs looking down to witness the fireworks.

Sanur went straight up to Lupe, who was trying to pack her company laptop into a bag. Sanur walked up to her, smiled a vicious smile, grabbed the laptop, and twisted it to where she had to let go or suffer broken wrists. Lupe cried out and jumped back. Aat came up behind him and took the laptop from Sanur. Sanur whipped the bag out of Lupe's hands and dumped out the contents onto the desk. He pointed out several USBs and printouts of confidential company financial documents. "Time for you to go to jail," he said very quietly. He held up his phone. "I got an alert that you were accessing confidential accounts. So, I called the police."

Two men in police uniforms stepped forward, and Sanur spoke to them in Thai. Lupe squealed and tried to fight as they put the cuffs on. One of them took pictures of the USBs and the edges of the confidential documents. Aat held up a picture on his phone of Lupe trying to steal the laptop.

Sanur stepped closer. "Do you have any idea how enjoyable Thai prisons are? I need a name. If the name is correct, I can make a request for you to be deported instead."

Lupe opened her mouth to scream, but Sanur simply held up a finger. "This offer will expire in five seconds. Five, four, three, two?" Lupe spit out two names, Somchair Buarin and Malee Choeyram. Sanur nodded, and they took her away. They heard her screams from the courtyard, and then things went blessedly silent.

Sanur spoke in quiet Thai to the workers, words of respect, of reassurance, of apology at the cobra in their midst, reiteration that their jobs would continue exactly the way that they were. He praised them for their handling of the situation and sent them all to an early lunch.

Tania and the teen boys soon came back downstairs, relieved that most of the photo shoot had already occurred. They sat down and covered the phones until it was time for lunch.

Sanur sent the young men away with cash from his pocket for lunch, and he said, "We can eat and then work out, or work out and then eat."

"I do need to beat the shit out of something," agreed Tania. Sanur laughed, swung her home to pick up her gym clothes, and took her to his gym in a new building near the office. He dressed in clean blue shorts, a red sleeveless shirt, and maroon trainers. Taia dressed in blue and gold, with pink and black trainers. It was a traditional bare-bones Thai gym with white walls. Sanur and Tania hit the jump ropes, weights, and the light and heavy bags before sparring.

Sanur watched Tania work with a lithe, fast Thai teen who had probably been sparring since age ten. Sanur was surprised at how good his woman was, how she moved her feet, bided her time to beat her opponent. Tania got a bloody nose and thought it was funny. Sanur's woman was tough, and he reveled in it. He got her a soft cloth from his bag and passed it to her, the pale blue turning crimson. She laughed. "Teach me not to sleep on the job."

Her sparring partner, Phet, was as hard as her name, which meant "diamond." She pulled on the tail of her French braid and said, "Americans. So easy to beat."

Tania stood, stretched, handed Sanur back the bloody cloth. "Not today, I'm not. I just lost a friendship, and I'm pissed."

"So?" Phet held up her gloves. "Are you going to cry, or are you going to fight like you mean it?"

Tania stretched her neck, felt it pop. Then, she raised her gloves. "I feel like hitting. So, bring it." Phet pushed Tania to use her footwork, to see false fronts and to move out of the way. When they finished, Tania gasped, drank water, found her voice again. "I think I have the funds to hire a trainer. Want to train me?"

Phet grinned. "It's either that or subject myself to bad fighting."

Tania snorted and climbed out of the ring. "Give this young woman my digits, love. I've got to shower, then I'm going back to work."

Sanur grinned. "That's my woman."

PROPOSAL

Tania and Sanur made it through the day and discussed the situation over pad thai that evening. "That little heifer didn't damage us as much as she thinks she did." Tania squeezed lime on her chicken and shrimp, then doused them in ground peanuts. "Lupe got into a snit and primarily was upstairs doing photo shoots we didn't need to stay away from me. She must have had some sort of alert to fight you about the new contract."

Sanur nodded. "I do not know what a 'snit' is, but I concur."

"A snit is getting coldly angry, like a child. Whoever she was working with may be able to try to get something away from us, but what? What we have is very unique, and there's really no way to damage that business except computer crap like, I don't know, a virus. You said you have some sort of hacker friend who did stuff that made that nearly impossible. That person still working for you?"

"Yes, I went to school with him. There were no alarms tripped, so I think yesterday was the day she decided to try to steal your power but wasn't expecting you to fire her. I think she thought you were a lot weaker than you were," said Sanur. "She thought you would not be willing to engage her. Petty anger is a sign of weakness, not strength.

Maybe she expected you to sell half the business to her to appease her."

Tania narrowed her eyes. "I get into petty arguments with my friends all the damn time. I did to her exactly what I do with them; I wait them out. There's usually an apology by the next day at the earliest, a week at the latest. She had about two more days before I was expecting a full apology." She sighed. "Who am I kidding? She would have had to apologize for an entire checklist. I was trying to be professional. I think I crossed the line into stupid." Tania grabbed a shrimp with her chopsticks.

Sanur le a bit of his anger over how Tania had been treated show in his eyes. "This shows that you can't trust everyone to behave the way in which one is used to people behaving."

Tania rolled her eyes. "I should have known that one by now." Tania picked up noodles with chopsticks from her bowl and stuffed them into her mouth.

"I didn't see this coming either. No one ever expects someone to behave quite so unprofessionally. Looking back, I can see the pattern, her shutting down. She was listening to those who were trying to get into our company. That is unfortunate." He sighed. "I still own just over half the company. I'm going to end up sexually harassing you."

Tania let out a laugh. "So, let's get married. Then what's yours is mine and what's mine is yours. We'll split the company down the middle or leave me at fifty-one percent so I can make all the day-to-day decisions."

Sanur looked directly into Tania's eyes. "Tania, among my people, this is not a joking matter. This is also not some medieval thing where we marry to handle joint property and businesses. My family has been doing that for centuries, but I decided I wanted more a long time ago. You would be marrying millennia of tradition, honor, and the network of responsibilities far greater than anything you've seen before. It's going to be upsetting, disturbing, and more work than either one of us can handle alone, even with my valet."

Tania stared at him, slack-jawed. "You make it sound like you are royalty."

Sanur nodded. "To all intents and purposes, I am." At her raised eyebrows, he said, "Take away your Western thoughts. There are no castles. None of us drive Ferraris. Or have suits of armor in the hallways."

Tania grinned. "You don't drink champagne with diamonds in the glass?" She knew Sanur wouldn't get the reference to the 2001 version of the song "Lady Marmalade."

He shook his head. "Why would anyone do that? No, we are...well hidden. We do not want paparazzi or to...influence others. We are not on social media." He shuddered.

"I see." Tania sipped her tea. "Actually, I don't. You're hidden royalty?"

"From an ancient line. We have people that we help." Tania nodded. Things suddenly made more sense. Apparently, his people had helped people for thousands of years. He was just continuing what his people had always done.

He ate another piece of chicken, then said, "I've already called someone to take care of the Somchair and Malee problem, one of my people. A woman, an old family friend and distant relative. I believe you would call her a third cousin."

Tania grinned. "Will she leave a trail of bodies in handcuffs, ready for prison, in her wake?" she asked, gleefully.

"No," said Sanur, taken aback. "You have a bloodthirsty side I wasn't expecting. I find it alarming and alluring at the same time."

Tania laughed. "Acceptance. I accept you differences, and you accept mine."

"There is a problem with too much acceptance."

"Yes, there is. You can accept your way into being a doormat, or you can accept what is around you until the point that your brains fall out, or when you let yourself or other people get hurt. Well, listen up. This is my family this woman, and whoever the hell is pulling her strings, has hurt. That will not be tolerated. And no, I do not want to marry you out of some medieval urge to live in your damn castle. Your home isn't some freaking showcase on a golf course, or a giant mansion. It fits into its surroundings, and it's beautiful. Understated."

Sanur put down his chopsticks. "Understated is our way."

"I know you have all sorts of money and property and all that sh—stuff, and you absolutely should make me sign some sort of prenuptial agreement. Get the lawyer on it. I have no intention of taking away what your family has built for, from what you've said, centuries. I can't guarantee I won't do something stupid and lose at least some of it, because I don't know what the hell I'm doing. I do want to be protected, so buy me a damn house in Bali or something for if we break up. You can have your life, I could have mine, and we will lick our wounds and continue."

Sanur looked at her in shock. "A marriage based on the idea of it disintegrating is not ideal for the start of a marriage."

Tania shrugged. "We have kids, which is kind of weird because we're not married yet and I haven't given birth." Sanur tried not to choke. "Although I'm relatively sure they would survive whatever the hell life throws at them. I would like for them to be taken care of, their educations, loans for apartments and houses when they graduate, then work to start a business or continue with the ones we already have. I don't want our kids getting spoiled, but they deserve better than the absolute shitstorm life has given them so far. If something nasty happens, we take care of the damn kids first, because I'm an adult and I can take care of myself."

Sanur realized that he was truly in love with this blunt, fierce woman in front of him. "The orphans come first," he agreed quietly. "And I understand protecting your assets from irresponsible behavior or simple mistakes. But I must train you in what I know, which will be intensely difficult, especially when we are trying to run several companies already." Sanur sighed. "But, as my majordomo has pointed out to me many times, apparently I am not very good at doing things the easy way."

Tania laughed. "Kandace says that there is the easy way, the hard way, and a no-way-in-Hades way. She says I'm the queen of doing things in some way I have to turn myself into a pretzel to get out of it."

She put her chopsticks down on the edge of her plate. "I love you, and I've known you for nearly a year. We built up a very strong friendship before we got involved. Hell, we even waited some more to be sure that we weren't doing anything wrong." Tania reached out, grabbed his hands in hers. "I've seen what kind of man you are, and I've seen you handle a truly wretched situation with intelligence and dignity. I didn't call the police on that heifer because I didn't think things had gone that far, but you saw what I couldn't."

Sanur opened his mouth, but she leaned forward and kissed him, then continued. "I love you, I love being with you. I love the company, I love the kids. Most of all, I love you. You are an integral part of my life now, and I can't imagine being separate from you. Yes, we have a crazy life. We can't watch more than one movie without interruption. Our night together was amazing. And delightfully uninterrupted."

He choked. "I am so sorry. We have had difficulties. I believe they are the pains of building structure. Once the structure is made, the problems will minimize."

Tania shrugged. "I really don't know of anyone who doesn't have a busy life. Yes, we apparently have someone or some people after us. I have never backed down from a fight in my damn life, and I will not back down now. If you don't think getting married will make things safer or better for us, or you just don't want to get married, tell me now."

"This is not how my kind makes marriage proposals. We don't make them at food stalls on busy streets with motorcycles zipping by. We do them with offers of gifts to show our great esteem and promises of love and respect, and we light incense and candles and ring little bells."

Tania smiled, and it was like the sun coming out from behind the clouds. "I don't need that. It sounds beautiful and romantic, so we can do that if you want. I crave you, your skin, your touch. I love your laughter. My day begins when we are together. If we can't work together, then we can live together. Lunches and dancing and movies aren't enough anymore. I need all of you."

Sanur felt his eyes mist. "If it makes you feel any better, I've been selecting the gifts for the past month," said Sanur.

Tania laughed, and was surprised to find tears sliding down her face. "Well, I'm going to have to select some gifts. I'm going to have to ask Htet what to give you."

"I need very little, so they should be small gifts." He clenched her fingers, reached up to wipe her tears away. "You must also memorize words you won't understand. They make a prenuptial agreement moot. We join our lands, our businesses, our homes, and our lives. Deliberate mismanagement, infidelity without both parties agreeing to do so, adoption without the consent of both parties, and several other things are grounds for leaving one another." Sanur sighed as Tania stared at him as if he were speaking Martian. "Most of the old promises are no longer necessary in the modern world. But the old ways must be honored. They brought us to where we are now. If we do separate in the future, we will separate with love, trust, and joy that we have been together. We also ensure that no harm is done to each other in those around us."

"That sounds beautiful. I can agree to all of that."

Sanur stood and kissed her on each cheek, her forehead, then her lips. He swallowed at the sudden lump in his throat. "So, I will have Htet send over a phonetic spelling of the vows, and you will call him at designated times three times a day to practice. When he feels that you can get through the whole ceremony without stumbling, then we will have the ceremony."

"Okay." Tania wobbled on her chair, a little dazed.

"After the ceremony, I request that you move into our house. I'll get a car if you would like to be driven to work, but we both have scooters, and the neighbor's son drives a *tuk tuk*. We will sign a stack of business papers and divide up our responsibilities. I look forward to that day with all my heart and soul." He kissed her fingers, then turned and walked away.

Tania wiped her eyes, finished her noodles and her cola, and walked back to work in a daze.

Two hours later, she wasn't surprised to find an email with an audio file of a woman nearly whispering the words in whatever language that it was. In between telephone calls, taking over Lupe's duties, and making sure everything was going well on the floor, Tania memorized one word at a time, one phrase, one sentence. She wrote out her own phonetic version of the script by hand as the voice whispered in her ears. She had never heard the language before. It certainly wasn't Thai. It sounded very old.

The entire time, her mind was whirling. She wanted to invite Kandace and Corinne to the wedding. But what if she couldn't memorize all these whispered words? What if the whole thing fell apart? Neither one of them would have the funds to fly to Thailand; they had massive debt, too. She knew they would come running, hell or high water, borrow the money from some guy named Guido who would break their legs later when they couldn't repay the money, if she even hinted at a wedding. Should she ask Sanur for the money to fly them out? No, that would be asking too much. She had to make things equal. She sighed. She was making herself crazy.

She also had gifts to buy Sanur for their ceremony-thing. What would a shapeshifter like? Cases for his shed skin? She shuddered. He lived so elegantly, yet simply. He didn't need more stuff.

She was determined to be paid off so they could join together with her owning the business with no loans, even from his trust. So, using her own funds wouldn't work. Asking the man she would marry for the money sounded crass. Plus, both her friends had work, a lot of it, from what she could tell. They would drop everything and come, but they had their own enormous debts to pay, and she would be asking them to fly across the world. They would have to take a week off and be very jet lagged on both ends.

Where would she put them? Her apartment? They deserved the best. All that expense and travel would cause them exhaustion, worry, and heartache that wasn't necessary. It broke her heart. Maybe she could sell something? What? She thought about her fake Stratocaster and her tip money and smiled. Then, she made a call.

HUNT

The next day, Tania was in her office answering emails, going over the ceremony and chanting it with the woman's whispered voice, when she received a knock on her door. She turned off the recording, looked up, and saw a woman standing in the doorway who looked like a slightly miniaturized Sanur. She sported his long, flat nose, the cut of his cheekbones, the same honey caramel color of his eyes, the same tilt of his head.

"You must be Sanur's relative, come to find the people trying to harm him." Tania cast her voice so she couldn't be heard past the door.

The woman stepped inside the office and shut the door. "My name is Supayalat. You may call me *Hteiksu.*"

"You were named after the last queen of Burma, now Myanmar," said Tania, a little smug that she'd been doing her historical research into Sanur's family. "But if you want me to call you *Hteiksu*, princess, you need to call me *Rani.*"

"Do you consider yourself a queen? You are memorizing the marriage ceremony," Supayalat quietly observed.

"I take it you're not here to make small talk. What do you need?"

"I'm going to take apart that woman's desk." Supayalat referred to Lupe.

"The police were here and left fingerprint powder all over the damn place. I'm afraid the scene has been compromised a bit."

"Since Sanur paid for her housing, and Lupe is in jail prior to being deported and hasn't cleaned out the apartment yet, I've already been there. I found several fingerprints the police missed. I've also been to the places she had her meetings, and despite those lounge chairs having multiple people sitting in them and their being cleaned, I found some fascinating fingerprints."

Tania typed a note to herself to remember to clean out and release Lupe's apartment. It had never crossed her mind. Tania mentally slapped herself for not thinking of it. She was relatively sure that Sanur had, and had left the apartment as it was until Supayalat came to investigate. "I take it you are referring to Somchair and Malee. Sanur told me about them. Please, do whatever you find necessary to go after these people. We're not in this for the money, we're in this to help people. If you don't have that mindset, you can't make this business work anyway. They would just loot it and disappear, just like they did before." Tania tapped her fingers on the desk.

Supayalat inclined her head. "So you think it's both of them."

"A woman wouldn't have made so many mistakes, but I'll make you a bet it's her greed behind all of this," said Tania. "If you are relying on being beautiful and a demon in bed, that only lasts for so long. And you have to keep yourself in top physical and sexual shape for years. Grifters don't like doing that much work. So, they convince others to do the work for them. Are there actual demons?" Tania asked Supayalat.

To her surprise, Supayalat didn't laugh; she just shook her head. "Just the human kind."

"My guess is Malee and Somchair lived the glamorous lifestyle and finished off the money they stole from Sanur and whomever else they were ripping off at the time. My guess is that they're both also vicious, cunning, venal, and stupid in certain ways. I'll also make a guess that they're not doing this to keep some sick mother alive. If that were the case, one or the other of them would have simply asked Sanur for help, and he would have given it. So no, find them, and have them enjoy a Thai prison."

Supayalat bowed her head. *"Rani,"* she said quietly. "And, just so you know, I prefer *Mibaya. Rani* is more Sanskrit. We started using the term when we moved south and west. But it is the term that Sanur prefers to use."

"Hteiksu Supayalat," said Tania. "Update me if you have time, but I assume Sanur will take care of that." Supayalat inclined her head again, and then was gone.

~

Tania was pleased that they didn't have to do photo shoots for quite some time. Lupe's recent preference to be separate from Tania meant that nearly every product was in a photo shoot. Tania was now in a position to create ads, not design pictures for them.

Tania had kept her previous online marketing clients, working like mad to pay off the partial loan from the trust for her fifty-one percent of the business, so she would enter the wedding debt-free. Since Tania got a free apartment from work, and she very literally didn't have time to run around buying much of anything, she made the largest chunk of payment on her loan that she could. She would soon have to completely withdraw from both the band and her old customers, which saddened her, but the company came first. She sighed about selling her fake Stratocaster.

She grinned when she realized she could pass on her marketing clients to her trainees; they could build a second side business. She made a note to herself; Sanur would know better how to build such a side business, adding local Thai businesses.

Exams were coming up, and the high school students were frantically studying. Tania was overjoyed that she had made plans to deal with this. The students got time off, and everyone else took up the slack, including Tania and Sanur. They somehow got through.

During this busy time, Htet brought lunch every day to Tania and

Sanur, and walked Tania through the ceremony. Tania could remember longer and longer chunks. Unfortunately, neither man took anything she was doing as a joke, so she couldn't use strange voices to remember the words. She secretly used the timing of the 1980s hit "Hey Mickey" to remember the ceremony in four-minute chunks.

~

Supayalat came back with Sanur to Tania's office half an hour after Htet arrived. Both were silent while Tania worked with Htet to let the words roll off her tongue. Htet came over in person because she was so close to reciting it perfectly. While she was waiting, Supayalat cleaned her nails with the little knife she took from her boot. Tania grinned, took the challenge, and within two tries was able to recite the entire ceremony. "Good job, *Rani*," said Supayalat. "I will give you one of these as a liege gift during the ceremony," she said, holding up the knife.

"Make it a belt knife. I only wear boots when I sing heavy metal."

Supayalat raised her eyebrows. "Hair bands? You sing the music of hair bands?"

"Don't knock it until you've nearly paid off your debt. I make a lot of money in tips, and people write their phone numbers and stick them in the jar as well. I seem to have groupies." Tania grinned proudly.

Supayalat pretended to bash her head on the desk. She turned to Sanur, who shrugged. Htet had a faint smile on his face. "My liege, you would like for me to swear fealty to this one?"

Tania laughed from the bottom of her stomach. "What did you expect? I'm a crass backwoods girl. I will probably use the wrong fork in a fancy restaurant. I like walking around my house naked, something I can't do in the future with a valet living in the house." Both Sanur and Htet choked, and Supayalat snorted out a laugh. "I will be whatever I need to be, but remember, you may take the girl out of a country, but you can't take the country out of the girl. And, pardon the pun, I'm also mean as a snake when pissed."

Sanur grinned. "My woman is strong."

Tania nodded. "Damn straight." She turned to Supayalat. "Have you found those two outlaws yet? Those idiots ruined an excellent friendship. In addition to screwing over my man, both literally and figuratively, those scum-sucking turds turned someone I loved into a bitchy, whiny middle-school girl, and nearly got her put in a Thai prison. I want payback."

Supayalat looked down at her screen, then looked up, exhilarated, eyes flashing. "They're hiding in Bangkok. I'm going to go there and have them arrested. Would you like to come along after work?"

"Can we be married first so that I may protect her from prison?" asked Sanur.

Supayalat shrugged her shoulders. "You can, but that doesn't leave either one of you time to purify yourselves, and I expect you're going to want a honeymoon directly after that."

"Don't even want to know what 'purify myself' means," said Tania. "Do I have to hose myself down with holy water?"

Sanur doubled over laughing. Supayalat snorted. Htet kept his composure. "No, it has to do with incense and prayers," Sanur said when he could speak.

"This is not a wet T-shirt contest," said Supayalat, making Tania snort.

Tania's eyes narrowed. "You people are going to make me homicidal, suicidal, and every other -cidal there is, if you prevent me from going after those nasty people. They screwed up my friendship with someone I cared about, and they messed with this company. I own it, it's mine. I'm going to go, I'm going to win, and if they have any brains, they're going to beg to go to a Thai prison." Supayalat shrugged and flashed something at Sanur with her fingers. Sanur groaned. Htet said, "I will make the travel arrangements."

Tania stood up. "Meeting's over. I'll get my passport."

"I'm coming." Sanur's voice brooked no argument.

However, Tania had no problem arguing. "You have five...or six,

I've lost count...businesses to run, plus the wedding to plan. I understand that you have some very old ideas of how to do a wedding. I don't care how we're married, just that we are married. We can get there and get right back. We may even be back tonight. Plus, if they see you, they'll run." She kissed him. "See you soon."

Sanur groaned. "I used to be known for my sanity. You make me insane."

"Supayalat will get us in and out. Besides, they're grifters, and not even particularly intelligent ones."

Supayalat sighed. "Yes, my liege."

Sanur nodded. "See that you do." He sighed. "I can deny you nothing."

Tania grinned. "I'm worth it."

Sanur sighed. "Yes, you are." He kissed her again, and then she rushed out. "I may regret this."

Htet smiled. "I think she may surprise you. She is small but fierce."

Sanur puffed out a laugh. "That she is."

~

"*R*ead this," said Supayalat in the *tuk tuk* on the way to the airport. She handed Tania a tablet. The wait at the airport, then flight to Bangkok were both so short that Tania barely had enough time to read the dossiers. There was nothing in them that would make anyone think that those two would turn out to be grifters.

Sanur's friend Somchair had been going to private schools on scholarships, worked three small jobs to pay for the food, housing, and tuition that the scholarships he had cobbled together didn't cover. Sanur had put Somchair in a position to finish off school without going into debt and having to work only one job instead of three.

After school, Desak and Ketuk went to Bali and started a profitable hotel business there. Sanur took his friend Somchair back with him to Thailand. Sanur discovered a way to use an import/export business to help artists in the places he loved.

Somchair was handsome, with a square jaw, flat face, long nose, and eyes that seemed to miss nothing. His smile seemed kind. Tania tapped the tablet. She spoke in a very low voice, nearly a whisper. "There's nothing here that screams, 'Hello, I'm a grifter and I'm going to steal all your money!'"

Supayalat's voice sounded like little more than a hiss, but Tania understood every word. "Our family knows something about courtiers. They are nothing new to us. Somchair did not hang on Sanur's every word, he didn't ask for everything he wanted. He refused gifts, even had little spats with Sanur. It seemed to be a genuine friendship as opposed to hooking himself to someone else's star to rise in the world."

Tania turned over the word *courtier* in her mind. This was a whole new world to her. Supayalat explained at Tania's confused expression. "Our family is used to this sort of thing. As long as a courtiers align themselves with our best interests, everyone benefits. Someone who would not have had a chance to rise in the world can rise much higher and can take advantage of some magnificent opportunities. If that person no longer wishes to align with us, the person can simply withdraw or manufacture a falling-out. As long as we are never harmed by this association, it is not a problem."

"I don't like being used," said Tania. "We will not be having courtiers. We may have employees, we may have family. We may have friends and various states of being close or not close. But I don't like users, and I never will."

"It can be argued that you used those orphans to benefit yourself. There are employment agencies you could have used." Supayalat looked down her nose at Tania.

"I tried that. The girl they sent from the agency was a bubblehead who refused to type or do anything to risk breaking a fingernail. I volunteered at an orphanage back in South Korea, and I know damn well those kids often don't get a chance in life. I knew I could train them, give them a better life. If the orphans hated the job, or if they weren't cut out for it, they at least would learn English and some skills."

"I see." Supayalat's voice was as dry as paper.

Tania narrowed her eyes. "I've talked extensively with each of them. They're being paid far more than going rates even to start with. They are not slaves, they can leave at any time, and the Thai government knows exactly where they are at all times. I even paid for more education for them online."

Supayalat nodded. "And that is part of the old ways, taking care of one's people. You have an enormous responsibility to make sure every single one of your people is more than just fed, housed, clothed, and has proper medical care. Your people must also be educated, something rulers historically have not permitted."

"What? Why?" asked Tania.

Supayalat smiled grimly. "Stupid people are like sheep, easy to herd. It has historically been much harder to reign over an educated populace. They know when they are being herded, and when they are not getting proper treatment. If you do not treat them well, you will lose your head."

Tania snorted. "Glad you approve." Tania opened the other file. Malee's file didn't point to a grifter either. She grew up in a small apartment with her brother and sister. Her parents paid for extra English tutoring for all three children, and Malee went to two years of business school. It wasn't surprising that an educated, beautiful woman who spoke fluent English would end up working at an import-export company.

It was also not surprising that either man would fall for her, because she was a smoking hot beauty. She liked to keep her long black hair up in golden pins, she wore just the right amount of makeup, and she dressed conservatively in long skirts and beautiful blouses. Her smile was lovely. Nothing in her file said that she would want to turn around and steal money and run off with the boss' best friend after sleeping with the boss.

Supayalat tapped the tablet with a fingernail. "It's what happened after they stole the money that was interesting. The money went to the Cayman Islands after bouncing all over the place. I managed to crack the account, but the money had already been moved. Either someone is helping them, or one or both of them took Embezzlement 101."

Tania snorted. "You can learn anything online."

Supayalat continued. "Sanur is not stupid. There was a small sort of petty cash account and a larger account used for running the business. That account was only at about half a million dollars. They didn't get away with the millions this family has in trusts, real estate, and currency trading. He had no access to any of those accounts, and it's doubtful he knew about them."

Only half a million? Tania finally realized that Sanur had access to millions. Was he a billionaire? She pushed the thought aside. Her man may have money, but he didn't act like a snob, and he certainly gave back to the worldwide community. Tania turned her thoughts to their search. "According to these notes, you got them on facial recognition through airport security a few times. But you couldn't get a bead on them, so they were spending at least some of the money covering their tracks. Probably using overland transportation to get away from their movements being recorded."

Tania sipped her Coke, handed back the tablet. "So, they were home free, and had enough money to settle down on an island and drink pina coladas all day, if they picked a cheap island. Why the hell didn't they stay gone?"

Supayalat smiled a feral smile. "You don't screw over a royal family anywhere in the world and get away with it. There are plenty of people who will tell me whenever they pop up on facial recognition. Wherever they were spotted, I would be told, but I was too late. They hopped around like rabbits."

Tania was smacked in the face with the word *royalty*. No paparazzi in sight, thank the Universe. Under-the-radar royalty. She took in a breath when she realized he may be a shifter prince. She hadn't thought of that one. "So, they were idiots who lived the high life and moved around when they should have stayed put and ordered umbrella drinks. Why come back now? And is there a point to looting the company or destroying it?"

"I think if they cannot do one, they will do the other." Supayalat's eyes were flat.

"This shit is amateurish. Find someone in the organization, feed that person jealousy, get that person to fork over information, force or manipulate me to turn half the company over to her. Reads like desperation. I think that they ran low on money. They're not experienced grifters. So they went back to the source, the one person they knew that had money. They would believe they knew how things worked, and that they would be able to loot the company again."

"According to Sanur, this woman, Lupe, considered herself to be an introducer and influencer within the expat community. She had some successful introductions and was paid well and had a good word of mouth. However, she become greedy." Supayalat's hissing voice was starting to freak Tania out.

"And jealous of Sanur and me. So they hatched the idiotic plan to get information to suck the company coffers dry, stupid because Sanur has things in place, withdrawal and spending limits, all sorts of things after they stole from him. Even owning a majority share of the thing, I can't loot it because of the way it's set up. Too many alerts."

"I have seen the paperwork. Impressive."

Tania grinned. "That's my man. So when it became obvious that if Lupe was going to purchase part of the company, that whole you-have-to-be-out-of-debt-first thing must have thrown them for a loop. They probably didn't have the money to pay down the debt, and Lupe had to earn that money and pay it off over time. That must have made them grind their collective teeth."

Supayalat laughed low in her throat. "I believe it left them with clenched jaws. The jealousy was an attempt to push you into begging what Malee thought was your lover to hand over the keys to the kingdom. All three of them were probably enraged when you received over half of the business, and Lupe was told to wait."

"Then, Lupe had her meltdown, designed to have me cave in and help my very best friend get what she wanted sooner, or to have Sanur do the caving to please her. But she let her rage and her sense of entitlement push her into doing something so unprofessional that I fired her. I believe she didn't see that coming. She thought of us as sisters, and that I would be so weak that I wouldn't smash her into the ground for that little stunt." Tania's eyes went stormy. "She didn't know me very well, because she thought that I wouldn't fire her ass in a hot minute."

Supayalat agreed. "I think she went too far, and then she tried to get the information she should have gotten months before. I've gone through everything, and the only thing she could have gotten was information on some clients. The company credit cards the two of you were using had limits on them, and they didn't have direct access to the main bank account."

"After I found out about Malee and Somchair, I understood a lot better why things were so compartmentalized. I even agreed with it. Why expose yourself when you don't have to?"

"I went in the other direction, found out where and when she met our targets, traced everything back. This has been going on for at least two months. Your joining the rock band made them all think that you were stupid, easy prey."

Tania raised her eyebrows. "Glad to prove that one wrong."

"I've got snatches of conversation from bartenders, servers, those kinds of people. Sanur is getting a reputation as a very nice guy who pays his bills and helps poor people get a start. When I spread the word that these people were trying to harm him, the money I paid them for their information was just a bonus. They were quite willing to tell me everything." Supayalat ordered more colas for herself and Tania. Business class had its perks.

"So, what's the plan? Bangkok is a huge, bustling city. If I were going to get lost it's exactly where I would go. How the hell are we going to find them? My guess is they have multiple IDs."

Supayalat grinned. "They made the mistake of using multiple IDs to buy drinks, move around town. They were so busy trying to evade detection that they forgot that there are cameras. Not everywhere like the United States, but banks do use them. They also like to live a certain way, avoiding backpacker hotels where they could disappear quite easily. They are in a three-star hotel called the Royal River

Barge, which is actually built out over the river. I think they see the river as an escape."

"It certainly makes it hard for law enforcement to surround the hotel," Tania pointed out.

"Yes, but they have never seen me, and if they did see you, it was from afar. You do have a very tiny picture on your website, but you glammed yourself up quite a bit for that one. You can look like Little Susie Tourist at any time. They think in terms of money and power. They don't think that someone like you, dating a rich man, would ever consider wandering around Bangkok with a backpack."

Tania snorted. "Looks like I'm buying a backpack."

"Oh, you will be given one very soon. It's going to have certain things in it. Things I think you'll enjoy." Supayalat smiled slowly.

"If they get away this time, I'm going to hit you over the head with the backpack," threatened Tania.

"No, they're not getting away this time." Supayalat smelled like very sharp incense, and her smile was feral. She looked straight into Tania's eyes, and did a weird nictitating-membrane thing with her eyes, a hint of a vertical slit showing. Then, her eyes switched to a flat, dark brown. Tania shuddered, sighed, and ordered another Coke.

GIRLFIGHT

*T*he plane landed and they picked up backpacks from an airport locker. Tania opened her black backpack and took out a camera case. Supayalat opened the camera case and walked her through what was in it. "Sunglasses with bone-conduction sound so we can communicate, and a throat mic, which is the necklace in this pouch here. Put it on." Tania examined the black-and-silver choker necklace with what looked like onyx in the middle. Supayalat had one of her own, in a tasteful silver with a blue stone in the middle. Tania flipped over the choker, saw the circuitry for a throat mic, then put hers on along with the sunglasses. Supayalat slipped a small camera into her pocket. A stun gun went into the other pocket.

A *tuk tuk* driver took them to the same hotel as their quarry. The river hotel was beautiful teak and mahogany, with a sloped Thai roof. The checked in separately. Tania was dropped off first at a nearby souvenir shop. She dressed in very touristy cargo pants and a pale green shirt and used makeup and a soft billed cap to turn herself touristy.

Tania checked into her prepaid room on the third floor, one floor above their quarry. She had one of the smaller middle rooms, with little more than a carved wooden bed and a closet for her things. She took her time going through the backpack and found a toiletries kit that popped open which had a sprayer inside. She slipped the spray into her pocket. She also had a tiny camera that she attached to her sunglasses.

Tania was kind of pissed off about not having a gun. She'd known how to shoot since she was six. Unfortunately, her father had kept his guns at the shooting range, making it impossible for her to take him out that way. *He planned it that way,* thought Tania to herself. Deep in the backpack, Tania found a little stick that turned itself into a blackjack with a snap of her wrist. She amused herself learning how to move with it, how to snap it back into its smaller version. She also had a hotel map, and Tania set about memorizing it.

The problem was watching their quarry in such a small space. This was a three-story teak boat, not the huge white confection across the river. Tania looked out her porthole at the river traffic going by, and knew they'd have to nail the two before either one of them got picked up by another boat.

Tania went down to the lobby with its bar and restaurant and ordered herself some iced honey lemon ginger tea. She nearly groaned at the joy of drinking something so cold and refreshing after the short trip. She had to keep from jumping when she heard "on your six" hissed into her ear.

Tania use the bar's mirror to see Supayalat sipping some fruity drink three tables back and to the right. Directly behind her Malee and Somchair sat at a small table. Tania wanted to have their asses arrested then and there, but there was a bartender, a cocktail server, and a beautiful woman in a golden Thai silk dress serving appetizers. There were also guests at each table, two more checking out at the lobby, and three more people behind them waiting to check in. These were felons who might become violent in a crowd in order to slip away.

Tania watched the couple's argument. She could only hear snippets from where she was. They were busy blaming each other for how badly everything had gone. They were appalled that Lupe had ended up getting caught and were trying to figure out a grift to get enough money to get out of the country.

Stupid, thought Tania, looking at their tight faces. *Everyone else is relaxed, checking in, checking out, having a drink.* The couple behind her and to the left were figuring out what they wanted from the spa. Behind her and to the right, a Western couple was eating a fresh fruit salad and drinking umbrella drinks. Supayalat was reading the wine list as if it held the secrets of the universe. *The only people with any tension in their shoulders, tapping their feet, are the two of them.* Supayalat had a hand under the table. *I bet she's not playing with her napkin, but taking pictures of those two*, thought Tania.

Tania ordered some chicken satay, because the couple finally ordered. She relaxed, ate slowly, ordered another tea. The grifter couple shared a fruit salad and some umbrella drinks, ones with actual alcohol in them. *Damn, I hope they get drunk*, thought Tania. The two gestured at each other, obviously arguing in very low voices. Tania grinned, feeling like a secret agent.

Tania finished and took her time paying the bill. The arguing grifters signed their own bill, putting it on the room tab. *Bet they thought they were skipping out on that tab*, thought Tania. To her surprise, the couple went up the curving stairs to the second floor. Tania followed, taking the stairs on the other side of the room when Supayalat sent Tania a subtle signal with her eyes. Supayalat's *tuk tuk* driver showed up, along with two other men. They positioned themselves at the base of the stairs, and the driver followed Supayalat up. *Either they're hired muscle or cops*, thought Tania.

Tania made it to the second floor, stopped on the end, looked over the railing, and pretended to take pictures of a passing boat with her phone. Supayalat nodded approvingly as she and the large taxi driver knocked on the door. Supayalat spoke in a simpering voice in Thai, something about a hotel gift. The door opened a crack, and Supayalat kicked her way in.

There was a scream, meaty slaps, and a loud groan. A guest poked his head out, and Tania waved him back inside. His blond streaked hair and pale skin marked him as a tourist, so Tania mouthed "police raid." The man's jaw dropped, and his eyes widened. He nodded and went back into his cabin. Tania slid her phone back in her pocket.

Supayalat pushed Malee in front of her as she came out of the room, and the taxi driver/cop/hired muscle had Somchair. Somchair favored his right side, and his lower lip was bleeding. They were both wearing flexible cuffs and were scowling.

Malee was keeping up a steady stream in Thai about being innocent. Somchair looked absolutely furious. Head low, he look like a bull about to charge. He lunged toward the railing, and Tania stepped forward, struck out with a flat hand, and hit the man in the solar plexus. Muay Thai boxing and years of the Society for Creative Anachronism fighting against males with swords in chain mail came in handy. Somchair gasped for air, and Tania prepared to follow it up with a kick in the balls. The taxi driver minutely shook his head, and Tania stepped back to let them pass.

Malee lunged and started screaming in English. "You stupid whore! You are just some idiot American. You are nothing. He was mine!"

Tania just grinned and stood aside. She wiggled her fingers at Malee. "You ran out of money, and now you're going to a Thai prison. Good luck with that shit." Tania kept her voice low, menacing.

Malee lunged again, literally snapping at Tania with her teeth. Tania stepped back. "Bitch, please. What do you think you are, a snapping turtle? I had one when I was seven."

The woman screamed and launched herself at Tania again, but Supayalat was having none of that. She pushed the woman to the edge of the stairs, and said, "Either walk, or fall on your face. Pick one. If you're still pretty, someone in the prison may help you." Malee realized that Supayalat was deadly serious and walked down the stairs rather than trying to get away.

Tania waved goodbye, went down to the landing, and watched two cop cars pull up to the end of the pier. Tania did a little happy dance and went to get her things. Tania mourned a bit as she slipped the expanding weapon far back into the case, then shrugged and put it back in her pocket.

"Going to be gone for a while," hissed Supayalat into her ear. Tania was surprised she could make out the words with the wailing of the sirens and the sound of the motorbikes flowing by. "I have informed our king of our success. Stay there, and I will be by to pick you up for the airport. Don't leave the premises, because I can't get my man back to you. The police want him as a witness to some rather insane behavior."

Tania slipped the little weapon out of her pocket and back into her luggage. "I will stay put. It is beautiful here." Her ear went silent, and she stepped outside to the railing. Tania took the camera out, went out to the railing, and then took real pictures of the river. It was, in fact, quite beautiful.

Tania finished taking pictures and sent them to Corinne and Kandace. She looked at her nails and found them ragged. So she booked a massage, then a manicure and pedicure, and had her hair washed, trimmed, and put in a long ponytail in the back of her head. Tania checked out, had a leisurely dinner and paid for it, checked out of the hotel, and walked out to the end of the pier. Minutes later, a hot and exhausted Supayalat got out of a cab, then stood quietly.

"Give me your room key. I will gladly get your luggage for you. Do we have time to be sure you're fed and watered?"

Supayalat laughed. "I'm not a plant, but I'll order before I take a very fast shower and get my own luggage." Tania walked in and sat back down at a table while Supayalat went upstairs, came back down and checked out, then devoured samosas and a hearty Thai soup. Supayalat went through half a carafe of water and paid the food bill.

They took another taxi to the airport. "I'm keeping the luggage. Do we have to go to a mailing place so I can mail a little tool to myself?" Tania slipped the small weapon out of her pocket.

Supayalat took it from her and slipped it back in Tania's backpack. "It will be fine. They'll just think it's a dildo." Tania burst out laughing.

Supayalat handed her back the tablet. "Time to study. Property One is one of our most ancient palaces."

Tania looked at the screen at the triple spires, the golden roof, wings, the gorgeous stone carvings. "It's amazing."

"It's on a fifty-year lease. Monks on the right, teaching martial arts. Monks on the left, different sect, teaching yoga. They will jointly maintain the grounds, carvings, inlaid floors, and the like. They have several courtyards for practice and seven buildings in total."

Tania stared at the pictures, each one more beautiful than that last. "Amazing."

Supayalat took the tablet back, swiped, then handed it back. "Building Two, low-income housing for the blind in Bangkok." Tania gasped. She had a lot to study.

CEREMONY

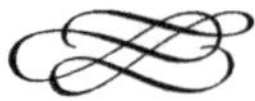

Sanur was delighted that Somchair and Malee had been caught. He did a little dance behind his chair and smiled thinking of dancing with Tania. He sat down, pulled up a spreadsheet. His phone beeped, and he picked up the line. "I'm Nim, man. I'm the guitarist? For Josie's band? You gave me your card once."

"Of course. How may I help you?"

"Josie, well, she kind of quit. She sold me her guitar. I don't see why she would need money. I gave her all I had."

Sanur sat up straight. "I'll buy it for twice what you paid." *What did his fierce woman need, and why didn't she just ask him for funds?*

"Cool, dude. She mentioned friends and a wedding."

Sanur sat there, stunned. "I...thank you, that helps. I'll transfer you to Lawan. She'll send someone with money who will pick it up."

"Naw, man, I'm in a coffee shop about five minutes from your office. Didn't want to interrupt your day."

"Come to my office. And...thank you."

. . .

he transaction didn't take long. The rocker's hair stood on end, and he looked exhausted. "I'm sorry to lose Josie. We've been auditioning, but no one's like her."

"No, no one is like her," said Sanur, shaking the man's hand. "I'm sure we'll come to see the show sometimes."

"Anytime."

Sanur checked, and found two open-ended plane tickets in the names of Kandace Walker and Corinne Jackson to Chiang Mai. Ah, his wife wanted to fly her friends to the wedding. Why not ask? Then he checked the trust account where she paid back the loan. The balance stood at exactly one percent left. He saw it, then. She wanted to be independent. To enter the marriage with no debt, as an equal partner.

He found the numbers to their cell phones in Supayalat's report. He sent them a text for a group call, and got a buzz back nearly immediately from Corinne, a bit later for Kandace. They agreed to a time. He settled into work, and got a great deal done before the call.

~

oth women were prompt. Both were also in jeans and logo shirts. Kandace's said "Climb" with a kitten climbing a wall. Corinne's said "Girls Code" and had an anime warrior girl slaying a computer with a line of lightning code. Kandace's red hair was pulled back, and Corinne's black hair in a braid. "So you're the mysterious Sanur. You are fine," said Corinne, looking him up and down.

"I am pleased I am adequate." Sanur tried not to blush.

Kandace laughed. "She means you're hot. Handsome. Pleasing to the eye." Sanur coughed, and sipped some tea.

Corinne waved a hand. "Let's cut to the chase. I've got clients every which way."

Kandace leaned forward and narrowed her eyes. "We want an upgrade. And a direct flight. And a wedding date."

Sanur sighed. "I didn't buy the ticket. Tania sold this to pay for your ticket." He held up her guitar.

Corinne gasped. "She sold it? Why?"

"To pay for our tickets, doofus." Kandace dropped her jaw. "She paid you off, didn't she?"

"She did. She wanted to be equal in the company. She...," Sanur discovered he had tears in his eyes.

Kandace nodded. "Ah. And how soon did you want to get married?"

"I will marry her at any time. We can marry tonight. I know she wants you there, so we can delay, but not by too much. There is...something I haven't told her. A gift for us. I will raise them on my own if I must...,"

"Puppies! You got puppies!" Corinne gasped, and clutched her chest.

Kandace narrowed her eyes. "No, that's not it, is it? You are apparently more than just rich."

"I'm...much more." Sanur bowed his head. "I must continue the line. Before, I went to a clinic, for...for my kind. Someone accepted. She did not inform me until very recently that things had...progressed well. She is much farther along than I had thought."

Kandace's voice was flat. "Does she want to keep the baby?"

Corinne looked shocked. "Baby? What baby?"

"No, she does not, and the pregnancy is dangerous. She has chosen to continue. After the birth, I will be a father. I want Corinne to be a mother, if she wants."

Kandace stared. "She will want. Very much. And be terrified as hell. Her mama was a dishrag and her grandma a...,"

"A piece of work." Corinne cut off what Kandace was going to say. "Baby? I want to see the baby! How far along is she?"

"Eight months. And she's having twins."

Both Kandace and Corinne jumped up. Corinne squealed, her hands over her mouth. They started talking to each other. "You get the registry going, and I'll figure out how to get us over there," said Kandace to Corinne.

Corinne nodded. "She'll need two of everything."

Sanur held up a black credit card. "Use this."

"You have to marry her now. Those babies can come anytime." Kandace stared at Sanur, face taut.

"But we won't be there!" Corinne stomped her foot.

"Would you rather be at the wedding or help with the babies?" Kandace asked.

"Babies," said Corinne. Tears streamed down her cheeks.

"You will be there virtually," promised Sanur.

"Give our girl back her money, and buy us a first class ticket to Chiang Mai," Kandace ordered Sanur.

"Bali. The woman is in Bali. You could come for the second half of our honeymoon." Sanur smiled. These were excellent heart-sisters.

"Give us that damn card number, and I'll get it done," said Kandace. Sanur rattled it off.

Corinne dried her tears. "She has Miss Amelia's pearl earrings for something old. She needs something borrowed, something blue, and something new. For the wedding."

"We have crowns. Then we return them to the vault. They will be borrowed, in a way," said Sanur. "I will think about the other things."

"Crowns? Who the hell are you?" asked Corrinne.

"I am a king of my people," Sanur said, simply. "From an ancient line that no longer rules...openly."

Corinne's jaw dropped. Kandace nodded. "Tania...will be a queen?"

Sanur nodded. "She always has been."

"Ohmigod." Corinne smiled.

Kandace nodded once, hard. "Okay, I'll handle it from this end. Four days? Five?"

"Five. I will send you the name of a hotel next to my friends' hotel. They will not have room, and the other one has a bigger buffet and a swim-up bar."

"I like." Kandace grinned. "I'll text you with the details."

"See you at the wedding!" Corinne said. Sanur bowed, and they were gone.

~

When they landed in Chiang Mai, they took a *tuk tuk* to Sanur's house. Everyone from work was there. The girls drew Tania away, laughing, exclaiming over her beautiful silver nails. They slid her into a golden silk top and a skirt that tied tight around her waist, heavily embroidered in gold, silver, and blue. They took her hair down and put it back up in little clips, and slipped silver sandals on her feet, exclaiming over her silvery pedicure. Tania looked in the mirror; she looked stunning, shiny-bright. Pleased, she had the girls take lots of pictures on their cell phones.

Supayalat came from Tania's apartment. "Here are the earrings." She handed over the box with Miss Amelia's pearl earrings. Tania's eyes misted. Miss Amelia would have been over the moon. "This necklace is made with carnelian square beads etched with silver, a new one based on an ancient design. It is my troth-gift."

"I don't know what a troth-gift is but thank you. It is beautiful." Tania put it on, and it hung at the top of her golden silk top.

"It is my gift to the person my...family member chooses to marry."

Tania smiled. She had almost said "king." She inclined her head, and Supayalat did the same.

Achara stepped forward. "I bought this blue bracelet from a client." The beads were simple glass, but beautiful."

"Something blue!" Tania slid on the bracelet, and hugged Achara. "Thank you!"

Supayalat said, "The wedding crowns are borrowed from the vault." She put her tablet on the side table. "Come, let's get you ready!"

Tania went through the lines she needed to speak again and allowed herself to be fussed over. How did they know to get some-thing old, borrowed, new, or blue? This wasn't an American cere-mony, but an ancient one with its origins lost to the mists of time.

Once she had red and golden ribbons and flowers woven into her hair, Tania sat off to the side and ran through her lines again. The words were ancient, powerful. She had the gist of what most of them meant, after Htet and Sanur had carefully explained their meanings to her. She would be making vows much more complex than "To have and to hold from this day forward." These were how kings and queens married, and the words were powerful.

As the girls put on similar dresses in silver and took turns working on each other's hair and makeup, the sharp scents of nail polish and hairspray in the air, Tania contemplated exactly what she would be promising. She would be a queen, making sure each one of her subjects had what they needed to find their own happiness. She had to rule, because her husband tended to travel the world. This was truly an equality. Her job was to be sure that she had what she needed to hold and protect her people, her territory, and the secrets they kept. Her husband's people had ruled vast territories, nations, and kept people fed, clothed, housed, and educated in times when all of the above was much harder to do.

Tania went over the words again, as Supayalat led her into a small area with incense wafting into the air, lit pillar candles in silver and white, rattan walls and mats. There was a single chair, and Tania sat in it, her arms on the carved wooden chair arms. *This is a throne*, she thought. Supayalat held up her tablet, and Corinne's face came on it. Achara held up another tablet, and Tania could see Kandace waving to her. Tania waved back and tried not to cry. Corinne said, "We're here for you!"

"This is incredible!" Tania said. "I wish you were here!"

"We are!" Kandace said. "Just on a screen."

"What if I forget the words?" Tania asked.

"You won't," Kandace said.

"You look amazing, like a goddess," Corinne said.

"You are amazing," Kandace said.

"I love you guys!"

Htet came for her, in a golden silk shirt and loose tan pants. Tania stood and followed him. The ceremony was in a wide room open to the elements. There was a soft breeze that played with her hair. Sanur was in front, resplendent in a silk coat in white, copper, and gold that covered his arms, and went down to his knees. He wore dark blue silk pants and a golden shirt under the coat.

Tania came to stand next to him. There was a Buddhist monk on one side, and Htet on the other. There were two more monks on each side of the open door, one with incense, the other with bells. Supayalat put flower garlands around their necks.

Sanur began to speak the ancient words and took Tania's hand. Then, Supayalat put a red, gold, and silver crown on Sanur's head. Then Tania spoke her words in a clear voice, and as she spoke, Supayalat put a red, gold, and silver crown on Tania's head. It took a while for Tania to finish the words, then the monks prayed, rang the bells, and waved sweet-smelling incense.

Supayalat gave them stunning platinum rings in an ouroboros style, a snake eating its tail, to exchange, and matching snake armbands. The snakes all had golden eyes with ruby slits. Then Sanur turned Tania toward the gathering, and she held his hand at his side.

Then they had a ceremony about adopting the orphans. This one was held in Thai, and the Buddhist monks smiled widely as they offered up blessings and prayers. They formed a line in front of their new parents. Tania was able to follow along somewhat and copy Sanur's words, and kissed each teenager on both cheeks. Tania made promises to look after all of them, help them reach adulthood and strength and health, to look after their education, to help them with their children and grandchildren. In return, the adoptees promised in Thai to show honor to their parents all the days of their lives, to preserve and increase the wealth of the family monetarily and with health, knowledge, and happiness, and to have proper behavior so that the family's name may never be besmirched.

Everyone had such huge smiles, and there was some laughter afterward as everyone got in line again for blessings and prayers, and more bells and incense. Then, Sanur handed the Buddhist monks bowls with envelopes in them and paper boxes with heavenly scents coming from them, obviously food. The monks bowed and left, taking their prayers, bells, incense, envelopes of money, and food with them.

Tania waved to her friends, and wiped tears from her eyes. Kandace and Corinne waved and cheered, then they were gone.

"Don't worry, you'll see them soon," Sanur whispered into her ear. "I bought them better tickets." Tania laughed.

Sanur held up a hand. "I know that we all want to attend the party, but first we have the most boring of things to do, paperwork to sign. Each one of you now have lands, rights, and responsibilities." There were sudden gasps, and the room went dead silent. "Don't worry," said Sanur. "You have stewards who will help you with all of this, and I don't expect you to learn it all in one day."

There were several obvious sighs of relief, and a wave of laughter. "We own farms of rice and mangos. We also have many herb gardens. As everyone knows, Thai food needs a lot of spices." There was another ripple of laughter, because it was a child's job to pound those spices with a mortar and pestle into paste. "I think there are many more spices we can grow. The farmers have been working that land for many years. Listen carefully to what they say, I know that they are very open to making new profit."

Aat was the first to speak. "Father, you greatly honor us, and we will be stewards of our lands. But, can we do what we're doing now? We can easily go to the universities and become better stewards for the family."

"Of course, my son. Just understand, this land is not to be developed, except for the gardens and orchards. There are enough hotels, condos, and things for tourists to see and do. If you want to invest in that, you are going to have to learn a lot after university." Everyone nodded gravely. "No, Thailand must also have its natural places. This is one of the most beautiful countries on the planet, and we have a responsibility to keep it that way." Everyone nodded into the hushed silence. Htet brought out the massive stack of paperwork, showed the adoptees where to sign, then explained in detail exactly what they were signing.

Sanur drew Tania aside, drew her to a small table and chairs, and sat her down. The small side table groaned under the weight of the stack of paperwork. "Love, you don't have to sign this all tonight. If you want to, you can hire a lawyer to go over everything if you would like."

Tania smiled at him, then gave him his first kiss of the night. They were both wearing metal crowns, so it was more like their lips touched, but it was a kiss, nonetheless. She smiled again, and said, "We can deal with the lawyers later. Just explain what it is I'm signing, but don't get into heavy detail. If I fall asleep before the reception, I'll be quite annoyed."

Sanur laughed, and explained in a low voice in rapid English exactly what she was signing, where to sign it, and why. She found out about the trust funds for the use of family members only, the bank accounts in banks all over the world, the four nonprofits in addition to the housing and import/export businesses, and the farms.

There was one nonprofit for building solar, wind, human bicycle, and water power for people in third world countries using mostly recycled materials, except for the solar panels. Another fund paid for schools closer to children, so that they didn't have to walk five or ten kilometers or more to school, and backpacks and school supplies. And the foundation also built medical clinics in rural areas. Another nonprofit funded and found scholarships for children in third-world countries to go to medical school.

The last nonprofit brought the other three together, literally. The nonprofit built roads in rural areas connecting villages, schools, clinics, and people going to work. All along the route people could rent electric bicycles using their cell phones and return them farther on down the road, or back where they started. There were also electric *tuk tuk* rentals for people to carry goods, children, the sick and elderly, and whatever else they needed to transport without having to have an expensive truck. This business was accidentally making a profit, and was constantly expanding, buying more *tuk tuks,* and building roads with proper drainage. Villages grew as the foundation built roads, schools, and clinics.

The roads also had over- and underpasses for people and animals, and their narrow bicycle-path nature meant that they were cheaper to build and maintain. Unfortunately, they did have to guard the workers against warlords trying to demand money for going through their areas. More than one warlord was unseated by trying to prevent a road from being built by the people Supayalat hired.

The second set of documents were for an increasing number of properties all over the world where they were doing business. Tania was overjoyed to find the names of the property managers. She was determined to get in touch with them and be a backup when they couldn't get hold of Sanur.

The last stack of papers were about their shared lives and responsibilities that now included orphans adopted into the family. Sanur's kind were expected to procreate, and they had already done so with the adoptions. She found the part where they were expected to have a child of his own kind, and Sanur smiled gently. "Before I met you, I met a woman. A surrogate. Eight months ago, I did this particular duty. It was...clinical. I did not know of her...success...until recently. She does not wish to raise my offspring. I know we haven't talked about having an infant ...,"

Tania jumped up, and despite the heavy crown, she held him close. She whispered into his ear, with a low growl. "She better not change her damn mind. I may not know much about having shifter babies, and I had a horrible mama, but I know how to love, and to protect. I'll be the best damn mama this baby has ever seen." She kissed his cheek and leaned back. Then she slugged his shoulder. "That's for not telling me we needed to buy a bassinet."

He held up two fingers, and Tania's jaw dropped. She carefully took off her crown. He took off his, terrified that she would hit him again. She carefully put the crown on top of the papers, swept him up in a hug, and kissed him deeply. Everyone around them clapped, even though they had no idea exactly what had set Tania off. Before she was able to stop her own mouth, Tania turned around, and said, "We're having two babies! And we only have one month to prepare!"

Into the dead silence, Sanur said, "Surrogate." Then they were surrounded by clapping, cheering, and many smiles. Everyone promised to have a baby shower when they got back from their honeymoon and told them not to worry about a thing concerning the babies.

Htet carefully took away the crowns and locked them up some-where. Tania signed the rest of her stack of papers. Htet came back and slid the paperwork into fat envelopes. A motorcycle courier rode up the drive, took the envelopes, locked them in a briefcase, put the briefcase in a lockbox at his feet, and rode away.

Then, they all went to change. Tania went back to their bedroom, and mysteriously found all of her things from her apartment in their room and put away in a brand-new golden wardrobe. And, her fake Stratocaster was in a corner with the little amps. She covered her eyes, and tried not to cry and ruin her makeup. A comfortable pair of tan pants and a soft blue shirt were laid out on the bed for her. She put them on and put on silver sandals.

Then, the party started. Thai chefs made extraordinary food, both clear and coconut-based soups, fragrant jasmine saffron rice, crab meat dip with vegetables, pork salad, pan-fried fish, and several curries. The food was amazing and flavorful, with many bright colors.

Tania ate until she thought she would pop like a balloon. Everyone kept passing Tania more food. Kannika made a joke. "Remember, you're eating for three now!" There was a lot of discussion about cribs and baby clothes, teasing and laughter. The boys put their fingers in their ears and made noises when the girls started talking about baby blankets. All except for Aat, who said that, as a gay man, he would be the one making the selections, and the girls would just have to wait in line. They threw napkins at him, making him laugh. Sanur handed out the number for his black credit card again and rattled off the address of an online registry.

Finally, after the lychee with syrup was served for dessert, it was time for the presents. Htet brought out chests for each new adoptee. They each received keys to put around their necks, then each one knelt and opened their chests. Inside there were new cell phones, already pre-programmed. "The phones are loaded with all of the documents and books you need to study to learn how to run your lands," said Sanur in Thai.

"Great, homework," said Aat. They all laughed. Inside were the court clothes they had worn, black credit cards for travel with the

Thai Airlines logo, manila envelopes with descriptions of their lands, their managers, and all who worked there, along with a list of codes that were changed weekly for each office, cards with access to personal bank accounts, both checking and savings, in their names, and information about brokerage accounts, including passcodes.

Sanur explained, and said, "Each one of you starts with five hundred American dollars. The one that has the most money in their brokerage account in one year will receive double." The adoptees looked at each other, then squealed, screamed, and hugged each other.

They also had luggage like the one that Tania now owned, one of her engagement gifts, along with her new wardrobe, new clothes, and her guitar, amp, and picks. They had toiletry kits inside all of them that popped open to display more things than it would look like they could get in there. The rest of the case was empty. "Someday, each one of you will have to travel the world. There are passport appointments for you on the blue cards inside your suitcases."

They all fished out the cards and held them up over their heads. "I expect you to get passport pictures. There are places in the mall to do that. The paperwork is already filled out, and you just have to go with the pictures. Htet will go with each of you while I'm gone. Listen to him as you would listen to me. We will run your affairs until you are able to run your own. Do that as quickly as possible, because I've got too much to do and too little time in which to do it." They all nodded gravely.

Tania took a little box out of her pocket. She handed it to Sanur. He took out a tiny golden key. Tania took out a locket on a golden chain, held it up to the light. She flipped it over to show the keyhole. "Sanur always has the key to my heart," said Tania. Sanur kissed her gently, tears in his eyes. There were some groans and catcalls, and hugs and Thai bows all around.

Their children stood in line to watch them leave. Sanur gave a blessing and said a prayer in Thai, and asked them to please stay, listen to music, dance, sing, eat and drink, and enjoy themselves. "We have a plane to catch. This is Supayalat. She will be running the business where you are working while we are gone. She will report to us

directly, and I expect you to do the same jobs you're doing currently."
Supayalat bowed her head. Their children bowed back.

Tania spoke up. "I expect everything will still be there when we get back." They all laughed. Tania and Sanur took off their garlands and handed them off to the eldest boy and girl, Aat and Kannika respectively, who took them reverently.

Tania cracked jokes about this being the third time she went to the airport in the same day. She made sure she had her passport, and so did Sanur, along with both their rolling bags. A *tuk tuk* arrived to take them to the airport, and they waved goodbye to their family.

HONEYMOON

They took a first-class flight to Bali. They held hands and talked about their new life together. They drank champagne, unable to eat after the huge feast they just had. They slept, holding hands, then landed in Bali.

"I hope you don't mind, I do have a house here, but I think we would do better in a small villa with a pool for the first few days. We will have a maid, and a cook three times a day. We could stay at a hotel, but I think you'd rather have the privacy," said Sanur.

"I think that's lovely."

The taxi driver took them past the rice fields. Their villa was gorgeous, with a king-size bed, a huge rain shower in the bathroom, the sitting room and kitchen open to the outside, and lounge chairs by the pool..

The chef was there with chilled fruit with a chocolate dipping sauce, croissants with little pats of cold butter, and lime water. She was a beautiful woman in a white apron, black hair pulled back, a chef's cap on her head. "My name is Putu, and I will be your chef. I know that you are looking forward to your time together, but please take a few minutes and press a few buttons for me."

Tania grinned and took the proffered iPad. "I would be happy to do so." She sipped lime water while she chose the foods she loved the most and the ones she hated from a list, and went through a few breakfast, lunch, and dinner proposals. She made her selections and handed back the iPad. "That was quick and painless," Tania grinned. "We had a huge feast back at home, so we don't need more to be full tonight."

Putu smiled beautifully. "I have left drinks and snacks inside the small refrigerator in case you should become hungry in the night. Please, enjoy your food, and I will clean up for you." She disappeared into the house, and Tania and Sanur took turns feeding each other bread and fruit dipped in chocolate. Putu took away the dishes, and they went inside to change into their swimsuits.

They floated in the pool, kissing languidly. They got out, laid out on the sun beds to dry themselves, then went inside. They took a hot shower together and washed each other. Sanur reach down, slid his fingers down her back, kissed her. Tania turned off the water and surprised him by climbing Sanur and wrapping her legs around him. "What about a condom?" he asked in her ear.

"I am covered. I get a shot once every three months, remember?" Tania asked him in response. Sanur smiled widely at her, gripped her hips in his hands, and let her set the pace. He kissed away her pants and screams as she came again and again. He let himself go inside her.

They spent three days in bed, the pool, the shower, or being fed morsels by their celebrity chef. "You're expending a lot of energy, so I expect you to eat heartily, or more often," Putu said, with a huge smile.

Tania laughed. "Can we steal you away and move you to Thailand?" she asked, seriously.

Putu laughed. "I am already on retainer. As long as Sanur is not here, I can work in any way that I so choose, but as soon as the plane lands, I'm at his beck and call. And yes, I have been to Thailand quite a few times."

Putu lay down the tray of chicken satay, peanut butter dipping sauce, and little bowls of fruit, and put it on the little table in front of the reclining poolside chairs. She adjusted the umbrella and lit another citronella candle to keep away the mosquitoes. "Would you like more guava juice?" Putu asked Tania.

"I had no idea I love guava juice. Learn something new every day. Yes, please." Putu bowed and withdrew.

Tania snagged a chicken stick and turned towards her husband. "Normally, on vacation, people enjoy light reading, or in my case, science fiction space battles. I had no idea I would be reading *Baby's First Year* and *Twin Surprise!* and panicking. Hyperventilating, really." Tania put the chicken stick down. "And how the hell am I supposed to explain two kids to my friends?" She breathed in deeply through her nose.

Sanur held her hand. "They set up the online registry. And they will be here to help."

Tania's jaw dropped. "No one told me!"

"To be fair, you were on planes most of the last twenty-four hours. And twins tend to come early."

Tania started hyperventilating again. "They do? And do you care that it's one boy and one girl? Two different eggs. I guess snakes lay lots of eggs!"

Sanur reached over and rubbed her shoulder. "I am delighted. We get one boy and one girl, which is absolutely perfect. The problem is, they're probably going to be fighting a lot. They are snakes, always looking for dominance, being sneaky, trying to determine the best way to get what they want."

Tania laughed through the tears that spilled out of her eyes. "That sounds like me and the girls back home. I kind of think being a holler girl set me up for being a mom to baby snakes." She wiped her eyes, and then attacked her food with gusto, making Sanur laugh.

They finally figured out where the beach was and took a long walk in the surf, holding hands. They ate tandoori chicken pizza at a beachside restaurant, then Tania dragged him to a club for dancing. After that, they went back and forth between mornings in the bed, breakfast and lunch by the pool, and sunsets on the beach, with dancing followed by midnight swims.

On the fourth day, they took a blue taxi to the other side of the island to meet Sanur's heart-brothers. Their hotel was small, beautiful, by the sea. They met his brothers at the poolside bar. Ketuk was tall, with a wide smile. He embraced Sanur readily. "Brother!" he said. "You did not say she was so pretty!" Ketuk embraced Tania.

Desak was wide, meaty, with huge hands and a kind smile. "Brother!" He enveloped Sanur in a hug. "Tania, you are more beautiful than my brother has said. Surely, this marriage is wonderful!" He enveloped Tania in a hug. Tania felt tiny with bird bones compared to his huge arms.

They sat at a table, and a server in a beautiful blue dress rushed to bring them cool lime tea. Guests looked like parrots in their brightly colored swimsuits as they splashed in the pool, reggae music playing in the background. The beach had couches, tables, umbrellas, awnings, and servers bustling about with drinks and platters of food. "You have a beautiful hotel," Tania observed.

Desak belly-laughed. "We are full even in the rainy season!"

Ketuk grinned. "It is so crowded that your new husband chose his own place. It is much quieter. And, he did not want to throw a guest out of their room!"

Sanur shrugged. "I would not displace another honeymooning couple. My brothers, we have family matters to discuss. When Tanya and I married, young people my wife brought into our business, they were orphans. We adopted them. You now have many nephews and nieces!"

They were halfway through the appetizers when Desak and Ketuk were satisfied with all the pictures and stories of their new nephews and nieces. They finished their seafood on sticks, then they all dined on shrimp, lobster, crab, and stuffed fish.

They were dining on cheesecake when Sanur informed them of the coming twins. Ketuk spit out his drink, and Desak helpfully pounded him on the back. Desak got up and pulled each of them into a happy hug. "Brother! We need to discuss the gifts!"

Sanur waved the thought away. "You have helped me with my crown jewel. There is never any debt between us. You know that."

"Crown jewel?" asked Tania.

"Later, my love." Sanur kissed her.

Tania let him get away with not telling her. What need did she have of beads and baubles? She had Sanur! And his very huggy brothers. Her stomach dropped again as she thought of being a mother. But now she was excited, too. The brothers' joy had rubbed off on her. She thought of Miss Amelia, and realized she had the best example of motherhood there was.

Sanur's friends told tales of late-night sneaking out. Ketuk said, "Our boy is what he is. We got him out, first in the orphanage, then the boarding school."

Desak laughed. "We told the dean he had an anxiety disorder, and he needed to be alone to clear his head. He did get jittery if he couldn't spend time as a python, so they believed us!"

"Speaking of that…," Sanur stood. "Love, I'll be back in the morning." He kissed her cheek.

Tania swallowed. Desak patted her shoulder. "We've got a real mean, old rooster, stringy. Attacked another male." Tania could only nod as Sanur strode away."

Ketuk said, "Are you wearing a swimming suit under your sarong?"

"Of course," Tania said, confused.

"Look over there." Sanur was talking to two women in sarongs. They hugged him. She stood, took a step forward, then realized who the ladies were. She started to run and crashed into a group hug. The women started to scream, cry, and talk over each other. Sanur slipped away and walked out to the beach.

"Our work here is done," said Ketuk. "Sanur's crown jewel is happy."

"Yes, Brother," said Desak. "Come, let us greet the pretty women."

Ketuk shook his head. "We won't be able to talk to them."

Desak held up a visitor comp card to all the hotel's amenities. "This will speak for us."

"Good idea, brother." They stood and walked over to the women, who kept hugging each other, tears streaming down their faces..

$\sim$

On the sixth morning, Sanur said, "There's something I want to show you." They ate a leisurely breakfast, then Sanur called for a four-wheel drive. The driver took them up the mountain road above a tea plantation, surrounded by rice terraces. The Jeep parked at the base of the hill. People crawled like ants all over a giant petal-like structure made of blonde and dark wood, entire floors open to the sky.

The driver hopped out, gave them hard hats, and put a hard hat on himself. "This is Nyoman. He speaks mostly Bahasa. That's Indonesian. He designed the most beautiful house in the world for myself and my bride. That would be you." Tania grinned. "We will be working hard, be under pressure. With so many children, we will be pulled in many different directions. We need a retreat, a special place." Nyoman pulled up the plans and rolled them out on the hood of the Jeep, then handed Tania an iPad.

Tania stared, then took her fingers and started moving the 3D rendering around. The whole thing was on stilts, made out of wood treated with wood stain, polyurethane, and fire retardant materials. There were Balinese petal roofs that rose above three stories. It had five bedrooms all with attached baths, a beautiful kitchen for Putu to cook in, a huge dining room, and a beautiful lounge. There were hammocks, cushioned lounge chairs, and even a small pool at ground level. There were gentle ramps in between the stories, rather than stairs.

Tania looked at it from every angle she could, then looked over at Sanur perusing the blueprints. "This is the most beautiful thing I've ever seen," she said, in a breathy voice.

"This home is for the Burning Season, when the rice farmers put the post-harvest crops on fire to add charcoal to the soil," Sanur said. Tania remembered having to wear a mask and carry asthma medication. A burning season is common in rice-growing areas around the world when farmers burn the stubble after harvest to add carbon to the soil. However, Chiang Mai's burning season could last for three months when people wore masks and were unable to see the sun during the day because of the smoke.

Tania looked at all the plans again. "I realize that we're going to have to be in Thailand for a while. Our kids won't turn eighteen quite yet. But this, this is magical. Beautiful. Understand that at some point, I'm going to come here and not leave."

Sanur smiled so widely that he felt like his face would split, and then held her close. "I am so glad you like it. Come, *Rani*, let me show you your kingdom." He took her past where the pour had already gone in for the little pool and up the first ramp. The floors, ramps, and roofs were already in, and the workers were building walls, installing pipes, electricity, and cables, and the kitchen counters were being built.

Tania was careful not to interrupt the laborers during their work while she walked around, wide-eyed and slack-jawed, stunned by the sinuous beauty of their new home. She went all the way up to the third floor, then walked back down the ramps.

Tania took Sanur's hand and led him back out under the trees. "You are going to love these trees," she said, quietly. "And I think our children will, too. All of them." She kissed him, and he held her close.

Kandace held Aye in a baby pouch on her belly while reclining on one of the sinuous couches and patted the little girl's back. The baby yawned, stretched, and fell asleep. Putu came, took the bottle, and switched it out for a can of Coke. She popped the top and put it in Kandace's hand. "Thank you very kindly." Kandace spoke quietly, and Putu was wearing silent shoes. Aye did not like to sleep, and she had a hell of a set of lungs.

Cetan was in his father's arms, sucking on a bottle. Cetan sucked down every bottle as if he had never been given food before. Corinne said, "Hand me the little man." Once it was time to burp him, Sanur handed the baby over along with his burp cloth. Cetan let out a loud burp, then waved his arms and cried, demanding more milk. Sanur passed over the bottle, and the baby sucked greedily. "I swear, I think this baby may be part pig." Corinne smiled down at the baby.

The babies were two weeks early. The giant petal house had been finished on time. The babies' heads sported shocks of black hair, fat faces, bellies, and legs, cinnamon skin, and almond eyes. Everyone was in love with them.

The Thai teens flew up, four at a time, to meet their new brother and sister and to exclaim over the house. Supayalat had flown up with the last group, done some sort of naming ceremony with some Buddhist monks, and flown back with the teens to run the import/export business. It was the burning season in Thailand, so Tania, Sanur, and the babies were not going back to Thailand anytime soon.

Putu circled the room with more drinks, careful to not go anywhere near the hammock where Tania was sleeping. Despite having a husband and two friends that liked to get up with the babies, the babies didn't like being separated from her very often.

Htet took advantage of a moment when Sanur wasn't holding a baby and brought over an iPad with some papers for him to sign electronically. Sanur read them and poked at them with a stylus, while Htet looked adoringly at the babies. Sanur signed the documents and passed the iPad back, and Htet made his soundless way back to the office.

Cetan permitted himself to be changed and rocked, but refused to sleep, and opened his mouth to scream. Corinne padded over with the baby to the hammock and lay him atop his mother. Tania embraced the baby in her sleep, and Cetan put his head on her stomach, closed his eyes, and slept. Corrine, Kandace, and Sanur all sipped their drinks in their hammocks or reclining chairs, lay back, and took advantage of the silent babies to take a nap.

Putu went to start dinner, and Htet took advantage of the quiet to do several loads of laundry and file all the business paperwork. He thought about making plans for Corrine and Kandace's return trips, but he suspected the women were not leaving anytime soon. Why would anyone want to leave paradise?

<<<The End>>>

THANK YOU!

Thank you for being one of my beautiful, amazing readers! I can't do what I do without you! If you liked the book, please leave a review! I read them all, looking to improve my craft so I can write more fun stories for you.

Thank you to my beta reader team, Lynda, Jodee, Swati, and Manasa. My editing team is amazing, Dawn & Rachel and iWordyNerdy, and so is my critique partner, Alyssa. Any errors left in the manuscript are entirely my own. Please let me know what they are so I can fix them in your online review! Or, you can contact me on social media at Facebook: facebook.com/lj.hawke, Instagram: instagram.com/ljhawke, Twitter: twitter.com/hawkelj, and my website: ljhawkeauthor.com.

Next books in the series:
Forever Claimed
Forever Wild

ABOUT THE AUTHOR

L. J. Hawke is an author, university professor, and an avid reader. She writes what she loves to read—paranormal romance, urban fantasy, and science fiction, as well as some nonfiction titles. She can be found petting her cats while writing, or with a backpack on her back, traveling the world--after calling the cat sitter.

One last thing...

If you enjoyed this book or found it useful, I'd be very grateful if you'd post a short review on Amazon. Your support really does make a difference, and I read all the reviews personally so I can get your feedback and make this book even better.

Thanks again for your support!